QUICKSAND

EMMANUEL BOVE
QUICKSAND

TRANSLATED FROM FRENCH
BY DOMINIC DI BERNARDI

THE MARLBORO PRESS
MARLBORO, VERMONT

Originally published in French as *Le Piège*
by Editions Pierre Trémois, 1945.
Copyright 1986 by Editions de La Table Ronde.

The publication of the present volume has been made
possible in part by a grant from
The National Endowment for the Arts.

Manufactured in the United States of America.

Library of Congress Catalog Card Number 91-61534

Cloth: ISBN 0-910395-69-1
Paper: ISBN 0-910395-70-5

THE MARLBORO PRESS

MARLBORO, VERMONT

CONTENTS

QUICKSAND

CHAPTER 1

Ever since being in Lyon, Bridet had been looking for a way to get over to England. It wasn't easy. He spent his days running about town to wherever he might chance upon some friend he hadn't yet seen. He patronized the brasserie near the large theater where the so-called "retired" journalists congregated, he strolled down Rue de la République trying to pick out familiar faces along the sidewalk cafés, he returned to his hotel several times a day in the hope of finding a letter, an appointment, in short, some sign from the outside world.

But within this mob that had invaded the city, amidst the difficulties everyone had to deal with, out among all these people who, back in Paris, even if they were acquainted didn't socialize with each other, there was no room for the least feeling of solidarity. You would shake hands, you would endeavor to look as happy upon the tenth meeting as at the first; you would sympathize together within the enveloping immensity of the catastrophe, pretending to believe that bad times really bring people together rather than set them apart. But once you stopped talking about the overall awfulness and tried to interest someone in your private little case, you would come up against a wall.

[1]

Evenings, Bridet returned home exhausted. To hold on to his room, every week he had to make as if he were leaving, hotels being reserved for travelers in transit. "It's grotesque, really," he thought, "not to have found a way to slip out after three months of this. It's even becoming dangerous." Everybody was winding up with the feeling that he wanted to leave. Nothing more certainly lays bare our intentions than a prolonged helplessness. By asking all the time and never receiving, you end up fostering the idea that you're the sort that won't ever succeed, that you belong to that slightly ridiculous category of people whose desires outstrip their possibilities.

On September 4, 1940, Bridet woke up earlier than usual. In the Hotel Carnot he occupied a small room, number 59, the last one. It looked out upon Place Carnot, opposite Perrache Station. All night long he had heard the sounds of comings and goings. Never had the French been doing so much traveling. Before daybreak he had heard the first trams. So life was going on like before! So there were still workers who went off to their jobs! And, as evoked by those cars clanking at dawn and by those iron wheels sounding upon rails, there was something deeply discouraging about that regular life.

The sun was up, but it hadn't yet risen above the houses standing on the other side of the square, and its rays, settling on nothing, simply spreading out through space, gave the sky a look of spring. All of a sudden, on the ceiling, a pale golden light appeared. Bridet recalled vacation mornings and felt a pang in his heart. Life was still as beautiful as ever. He too had the urge to travel. But in Avignon, in Toulouse, in Marseilles, would he find things any better? There was no air to breathe anywhere. Wherever you went you felt the weight of an ever heavier presence of police. Every officer was seconded by another, sometimes even by someone in civilian dress who, in his haste to assume his duties, hadn't waited for a uniform to be issued to him.

"I don't like it, but I've nonetheless got to go and see Basson," grumbled Bridet. Every day he told himself that he had to go to Vichy. He reproached himself for his procrastinating. He had spent the whole summer dawdling about villages in the Puy-de-Dôme, the Ardèche, the Drôme, hoping for something or other, and now he had the feeling that what he might have been able to do amidst the confusion that had followed the armistice was becoming more difficult with every passing day.

He had friends, Basson for one, Basson would see that he be given some sort of mission, a passport. Once outside of France Bridet would manage fine. England wasn't inaccessible after all.

"I've absolutely got to see Basson," he repeated. He would simply not let on to what he was up to. He'd tell everybody he wanted to serve the National Revolution.

"Will they believe me?" he wondered. He recalled just then that he had talked a lot, that for a long while he'd made no bones about saying what he thought, that even today there were moments when he couldn't hold back. Up until this point his loose talk didn't seem to have produced any repercussions, but now all of a sudden, with the time come to act, it appeared to him as if the whole world knew his plans. Then, to buck himself up, he thought that at bottom people don't judge us by what we've previously said—they themselves have said so many things—but by what we are saying at the present moment. He just needed to toe the Marshal's line the whole way. He was a wonderful man. Thanks to him the Germans had some respect for us. They rose above their victory. And we, for our part, rose above our defeat, which enabled our two peoples to talk to each other almost as one equal to another. That's what you had to say. Talking to a fanatic, you could even venture farther still. If every Frenchman looked deeply into himself, he simply had to admit, if he was sincere, that with the signing of the armistice he had experienced an immense relief.

"You were out on the roads and now you're back home," the Marshal had said. All Bridet had to do was say the same thing. He need feel no scruple about deceiving such people. He could tell them whatever rubbish he chose. Later, after joining de Gaulle, he'd make up for it.

Once dressed, he went out. One hundred yards away he entered another hotel to pay his wife the customary little morning call.

Hiding in the large mirror in the center of the lobby was the famous poster showing a tricolor flag with the Marshal's head drawn in the middle: the three-quarters profile to mark his modesty, the studiously refined features, the starched detachable collar, the perfectly squared képi, and that expression combining profound honesty, a slight bitterness, and a steadfastness that does not exclude kindness, which bad artists are so good at depicting.

Yolande had also found a room; it, like her husband's, was too small to sleep two. Indeed, Bridet wasn't too much put out by this. He was in such a state of despondency that he preferred to be alone. He had loved his wife very much but, since the armistice, without his clearly realizing it, he had drifted a bit away from her. All of a sudden she was having wishes, desires that were no longer his. She too had been struck by the catastrophe and she seemed to be discovering now that in life there were other things of importance besides harmony within a household.

She worried about her family left behind in Paris. She was impatient to see again people who until then she had not cared about. She constantly spoke about the little fashion shop she had on Rue Saint-Florentin and about her apartment, as if she had lived there alone. Bridet had felt that he had gradually become not so much a stranger in her eyes but one of those persons we are rather neglectful of, for love us though they may, they cannot be of any help to us. And, deep down, he considered she was right in judging him this way. Indeed, there wasn't anything he could do for her. So long as there had been an army, he, as part of it, had defended his wife. At present, he wasn't defending her anymore. He couldn't go in her stead to request an *Ausweiss*, he was unable to arrange for a mere room for her, or to find her a taxi, he couldn't send money to her family in Paris, or see to the shop, he could do absolutely nothing. She knew this, and she had finally got into the habit of relying on herself alone.

He sat down next to her. Until now he'd never made the faintest allusion to his desire to leave.

"Listen, Yolande. I've got to have a serious talk with you."

She glanced at him without seeming to notice that he was more solemn than usual. The lobby was crowded. They would have had to speak in whispers and to keep a constant look out.

"Come along with me," said Bridet. "We'll be more comfortable over there."

Yolande got up. They went and sat down side by side at the rear of the lobby.

"I've spent the whole night thinking," said Bridet. "I've got to go and see Basson."

Yolande kept silent. Bridet became heated. He had had enough. He was sorry he hadn't done this earlier. Now his mind was made up. He would go and see Basson. He would give the impression of speaking frankly with him. He would tell Basson that he admired the Marshal . . . He would ask for his support. Basson was an old chum. He wouldn't turn him down. But in the course of spending unhappy and miserable months together we say so many things, we make so many plans without anything changing in our life, that once we take a decision we all of a sudden realize that nobody has any reason to believe us.

"You're crazy!" she said.

Bridet answered that he had given it careful thought.

"I admire the Marshal," he repeated in a louder voice.

"Nobody will believe you," Yolande answered in his ear. "You really think people are idiots? You're going to get yourself arrested. Everybody knows what you think. You've said it often enough. Why are you going on this way? Why don't you want us to go back to Paris?"

The whole while he was walking aimlessly through the city, Bridet wondered whether he should go see Basson or not. There are some performances we cannot stage even when our future hangs in the balance. We cannot say that we like the very people we hate. Attempting it, our lies would be detected. So what to do? Return to Paris? Follow Yolande? Obediently show your papers to the Boches on crossing the Demarcation Line? See the swastika flying everywhere over a deserted Paris? Yolande said that the fact she sold hats to Germans who wanted to send presents to their wives didn't mean she was a bad French-woman. She would earn a lot of money and he who had always claimed he never had enough peace of mind to write a book, well, he'd get his peace of mind . . . It was sickening.

Yolande loved him nevertheless. She was ready to do for him what she would never have done before. Today, according to her, it was up to women to play the lead role, to move out into the forefront, to see to it that the men were forgotten about as a way of preserving them intact for the day they would be able to take up their arms again.

That evening, in his room, Bridet felt that he had a fever. He was on fire. Every now and then he thought he was about to start shivering. But he didn't get the shivers. The first appearance of this same sensation of being sick dated back to the month before. He constantly seemed on the verge of a dizzy spell, his eyes were already in search of a bench or a chair. But without his feeling any better on that account, no dizziness arose.

Outside the mistral had started to blow with extraordinary force. The sirocco, the mistral, the Genevan *bise*—in short, about all such dreaded winds there is something that sets them apart from ordinary winds, namely, how in a peaceful house the closet doors, the windows giving on small courtyards, even objects presumably sheltered all at once are set trembling.

Bridet made out mysterious sounds. "What to do?" he wondered. He thought he heard somebody behind the door. He couldn't help thinking about Basson. Perhaps the most disagreeable thing that can happen to a proud man is to depend on a friend he has neglected, a person we've never believed in, and whom events, by placing our fate in his hands, now seem to prove to have been right while proving us wrong.

Bridet fell asleep at last. The following morning he took the train.

[7]

CHAPTER 2

Located in a room at the Hotel des Célestins, Paul Basson's office had two windows hung with white muslin curtains. For a month Paul Basson had been working at General Headquarters of the National Police. When Bridet entered he got up and came around to shake the hand of his former schoolmate and old newspaper sidekick.

Bridet then experienced that sensation of discomfort we feel before a man with whom we shared the same dependent situation and whom we rediscover suddenly active and powerful. Standing alone on a desktop clear of all papers and files was a bouquet of greenhouse carnations in a crystal vase. Bridet sat down in an armchair. Never had Basson decorated the room he occupied as a bachelor and now the air in his policeman's office was fragrant with flowers. This detail betrayed a state of mind that gave grounds for worry.

"I came to see you," said Bridet, "in order to ask for your support."

"A very normal thing to have done. What are you up to these days?"

"Not much."

Basson glanced out the window at the park's lawns and trees. You'd never have thought that the armistice was hardly four months old. Like an undaunted widower he had started a fresh life. The house was still new. It gave you something of the feeling of being at an exhibition the day before the scheduled opening. This was natural enough after so great a calamity.

"Here's the story," said Bridet. "I want to serve my country. I want to be useful. The Marshal has taken our destinies in hand. We no longer have the right to ask ourselves whether we do or whether we don't like the man who is governing us. We must take him such as he is. As for myself, I'm convinced that Pétain will save us all."

At that moment a quite unexpected look of ill-humor showed upon Basson's face. He uttered two or three incoherent words, stopped, then finally said in a very chilly tone: "Don't talk about the Marshal."

Bridet looked at him with surprise.

"Why?"

"I'm taking the liberty of telling you this. Never talk about the Marshal. Never say that he must be followed. People will believe that you're against him. And I'd find that very disagreeable."

Bridet understood that he had been clumsy. The fact that he'd come to see Basson made it obvious he was pro-government. All explanations were superfluous and smacked of justification.

Basson went and sat down behind his desk.

"What do you expect from me?" he asked as if nothing had happened.

"Well, I don't quite know what to say to you now . . . I didn't think it was the wrong sort of thing to do . . ."

"Please, let's just drop it. What do you expect from me?"

"I told you that I wanted to serve my country. And I

thought that I could, for example, be sent to Morocco, to work at strengthening ties, as they say, between Metropolitan France and the Empire."

"Why 'as they say' ?"

"I don't know. Strengthening ties is an everyday expression. 'As they say' shocks you?"

"And why especially in Morocco?"

"In Morocco or someplace else. It doesn't matter to me."

"You just want to go away?"

"No. I simply have the feeling I'm of no use here."

"You're wrong. You can be very useful. We have a great task to accomplish. There'll never be too many of us for the work of reconstructing France."

"I share your view."

"You! You share my view!"

"Yes."

Basson looked at his friend the way a priest would at a café-concert performer.

"I didn't know you were so preoccupied with the future of the fatherland," continued Basson.

"I didn't use to be, but events have occurred and I've been changed by them."

"So, you want to reconstruct France!"

"I want to do what I can."

"Basically, you're not all that clear in your mind what you want to do."

"Perhaps you're right . . ."

"But there's one thing you do know: you want to leave France."

"No."

"You just said so yourself."

"I just said that I wanted to serve my country."

Basson held an automatic pencil between his fingers.

He was drawing capital letters on an envelope. And the whole while he talked, he seemed deeply absorbed by what he was doing.

"Do you really want to serve your country?"

"Naturally. If I didn't want to, I wouldn't have looked you up. I would have gone to live a life of peace and quiet off in the country, in Berry at my mother's."

Basson appeared to be struck by this argument.

"So then, you want to leave," he said.

"I believe that it's in the government's interest to send trustworthy people to the colonies."

Basson kept drawing.

"And Yolande?"

"She's in Lyon. We're both in Lyon. I already told you."

"Would she follow you?"

"Oh, I don't think so. You know she has a shop. She wants to go back to Paris."

"And you, you don't want to?"

Bridet realized that he had to tell another lie.

"That's what I may do if I'm bored at my mother's and I don't get sent abroad."

"What I don't understand is why you don't just do something for the newspapers. They're all right there in Lyon."

While uttering these words Basson opened and closed his eyes several times as if they were hurting him.

"I find them just a little bit disgusting, those newspapers. They're playing a double game."

Basson raised his head for the first time.

"What do you mean?" he asked.

Bridet dared not bring up the Marshal.

"They aren't sincere," he answered.

"Do you mean that they pretend to be with us and that they're not?"

"That's right."

"And that disgusts you?"

"Naturally. I wouldn't be in your office otherwise."

"That really disgusts you?"

"I've just said so."

"Yes, I know, one can say it."

Bridet grew uncomfortable. He glanced around. Would he be able to leave in a little while? Wasn't this the office of one of the heads of the police? Was Basson truly a friend?

"So Morocco is where you want to go?" asked Basson.

"Yes, I want to go to Morocco," answered Bridet, without thinking about what he was saying.

Shouldn't he have stated more clearly, a little while ago, that he was for Pétain? Basson's remark had stopped him. He felt that words were worthless around here. It was a bit the way it is in a courtroom. Nevertheless, matters needed to be clarified.

"You told me a little while ago," Bridet continued, "that you found it disagreeable that I talk about the Marshal. But you forget that it's been quite a while since we've seen each other. You don't know what I think. And I want you to know."

Basson smiled.

"I notice that you're nervous."

"I dare say. You look as if you doubt me."

"I? Doubt you? It's all in your imagination. You can be very sure that if I had the least suspicion about your sincerity, you wouldn't be sitting here in my office"

Bridet felt a contraction in the pit of his stomach. His instinctive reaction was to smile in his turn.

"You're right. I am nervous. I've had endless difficulties . . ."

"Yes, and what difficulties! I know what it's like."

Basson got up. As if preparing to go out he put his cigarettes and lighter in his pocket. Then he sat back down. It was Bridet's turn to get up

"Don't run off just yet," said Basson. "I've got something important to tell you."

Bridet sat back down. Vaguely anxious, he gazed at his friend.

"Something very important," continued Basson.

"What might that be?" asked Bridet.

"I want to give you a piece of advice, friendly advice."

"You want to give me a piece of advice?"

"Yes. And my advice is: be careful."

Bridet tasted his saliva turn bitter.

"Why?" he asked, feigning deep surprise.

"I'll say it once more: be careful."

"But why?"

"Be careful and don't act like an idiot."

"Is there danger?"

"You're going to get yourself into trouble."

"Me?"

"Yes, you."

"What kind of trouble? Tell me. About what?"

"You're smart enough to understand me. Now let's change the subject. Isn't Yolande going to join you here?"

"What kind of trouble? You must tell me what it's about."

"No, no, let's talk about Yolande."

At that moment there was the subdued sound of the house telephone. Basson spoke for a moment or two and as if Bridet were interrupting him, he signalled with his hand that he mustn't push the matter, that he would tell him nothing.

"Show him in," he finally said before hanging up.

Then addressing Bridet, he continued: "I have someone

[13]

I have to see. Just step outside will you, and wait a moment in the lounge? I'll have you called once I'm free."

"You'll explain to me what you meant."

"No, no, I already told you, we'll talk about Yolande, our friends, about everything but not about politics."

"Is it because of politics?"

"Don't ask me questions. I don't want to answer you."

Bridet took a seat in the lounge where there were already four or five people waiting. There was sweat on his forehead. His hands were shaking slightly. Lest this be noticed he placed them on his legs. They kept trembling. He hid them under his hat. What, he kept asking himself over and over again, what had Basson meant?

"I've done nothing," he was thinking. "Obviously I've let lots of people suppose that I wanted to go to England, but those people wanted to go there too. And besides there aren't all that many of them. Maybe ten all told. Even assuming there may have been some gossiping, that a file exists on me, Basson, who wasn't expecting my visit, had no reason to ask to see it. People may have told him I was a Gaullist. But nobody could give him any proof of it. I myself have never said in so many words that I was a Gaullist. I said I was going to England to join the Free French forces. That's all. No, Basson just got the feeling that I wasn't for the Marshal. When he told me that I was going to get myself into trouble, he no doubt meant that I was wasting my time working to pass myself off for something I wasn't, that it wasn't going over, and that in the end this act of mine would catch up with me. Maybe he thinks I've come to Vichy to spy. Or else, and this would be a lot more serious, or else, deep in his heart Basson himself may be a Gaullist. He may have wanted to make me understand that my admiration for the National Revolution could cost me dearly one day."

Bridet racked his brains to no avail, he wasn't able to figure out what sort of trouble Basson referred to.

"I'll ask him when I go back in and I'll insist until I get an answer, and if he doesn't want to answer me, well then, it'll be over between us. I'll certainly come up with some other way to leave the country. Nobody's indispensable."

Bridet was in the midst of his thoughts when a bareheaded man, rather youthful-looking, walked into the waiting room.

"Monsieur Bridet?" he asked.

"That's me, that's me," Bridet said, sitting up straight.

"Will you be so kind as to follow me?" continued the youthful man.

"Certainly," said Bridet, his tone proclaiming a certain self-satisfaction at being called ahead of the people who had arrived before he had.

"Has Monsieur Basson wound things up?" asked Bridet in the corridor.

"I haven't seen him."

"Excuse me? Isn't he the person who sent you?" asked Bridet, a trembling entering his limbs.

"I don't know."

"But where are we going? I mustn't wander too far off. Monsieur Basson is waiting for me."

"We're going very close by, over to Algerian Affairs."

"Oh, all right," said Bridet, involuntarily letting out a relieved sigh.

Everything fitted together now. Basson was a true friend after all. He'd given Bridet a bit of a scare, for no reason, for fun, a joke or on an impulse. Bridet now recalled that Basson always used to behave that way. He enjoyed refusing what was asked of him, appearing very reluctant and mysterious, and then after you'd given up on him you'd discover that he'd outdone all you'd expected of him. By George, he hadn't changed. "Watch your step, you're heading for trouble, wait for me outside in the lounge . . ." And then he would do what needed doing.

Bridet and the government clerk went down a long hallway, the rows of doors on either side bearing numbers painted on plaques. When one opened you got a glimpse of employees, typewriters and, stacked along the walls, enormous piles of paperwork and files which had traveled every mile of the retreat and from which important items must surely have been missing.

"Go in, Monsieur," said the clerk, opening a door and stepping aside with slightly mechanical courtesy.

Bridet then found himself in a room whose walls were covered with a tacked-on beige-colored material. There was just a table and one chair.

"Have a seat, Monsieur, I'll go and check if the director can see you."

"Which director?" asked Bridet.

"Monsieur de Vauvray, the director."

"Oh yes, fine . . . well then, I'll have a seat," said Bridet, who once again felt uneasy.

A few minutes went by.

"But hold on now," thought Bridet, "there's something I don't understand very well. Basson asked me to wait for him in the lounge while he saw a visitor. Where did he find the time to talk to this Monsieur de Vauvray? All this strikes me as a bit quick."

The door to the adjoining room opened and the government clerk, without coming forward, motioned for Bridet to approach. This other room was much bigger and had the look of a private office.

Monsieur de Vauvray—for it was certainly he—had his back turned to the door. His hands were in his pockets. He was gazing out the window as if, through shyness or fear of appearing ill at ease, he preferred not to see his visitors until they had made their way up to his desk.

"Sir, here's Bridet," said the clerk.

He turned around, in his expression the touch of surprise of someone who hadn't heard anyone come in. He drew his hands out of his pockets and went over to meet his visitor with a smile.

"Ah, here you are," he said. "Delighted to make your acquaintance. Sit down, light a cigarette." Then, turning toward the clerk, he added: "You can leave us."

The director was a young man, at most twenty-five years old, but unlike officials of this age, he didn't give you much of an impression of taking himself seriously. He was informal, good-natured, and you felt that in his entourage they probably viewed him as a real character. It was reassuring.

"I'm happy to meet you, Monsieur," he repeated, but this time emphasizing his words with gestures intended to stress their value.

"So am I, sir," said Bridet.

"Our friend Basson spoke at length about you." ("When?" Bridet again wondered.) "Needless to say I'm entirely at your disposal, but you ought to know right away that Morocco isn't within our province at the Ministry of the Interior. It's under Foreign Affairs. If you want to go to Algeria, I'm the person you have to see. And, in that case, I repeat, I'm entirely at your disposal."

[17]

"You're too kind," said Bridet.

"It's understandable. You're a friend of Monsieur Basson. I'm a friend of his myself. We'll be very happy if we can be of use to you in any way. When do you want to leave?"

"In two weeks. I'm not in any special hurry . . ."

"Really? I thought you were in quite a hurry, it seems to me that Monsieur Basson told me that . . ."

"No, quite the other way. I'm not in any hurry at all. What's more, I'll leave only if it's possible for me to do something out there. This is precisely the point I need to bring up with Basson again."

"Under those conditions, there's no hurry."

"No, there's no hurry."

"Well then, do you know what we're going to do? Since you're here, you'll go into the room next door, you'll give the young man you saw just a while ago all the information we need—oh, it doesn't amount to much, mere formalities, then we'll attend to everything that must be attended to and all you'll have to do is come by when you want to pick up your safe-conduct pass. You see, nothing could be simpler."

Upon leaving the government clerk's office Monsieur Bridet asked the usher to announce him to Monsieur Basson. He filled out a card and waited. The usher, card in hand, returned a short while later. "Monsieur Basson has gone out," he said.

Bridet took a walk and sat down on the bank of the Allier. It was a splendid day. The foliage was starting to turn. The sky was a dense and heavy blue and within that blue the sun shone with added brightness.

"Basically, I got what I wanted," thought Bridet. But he

did not rejoice. It felt to him that there was some menace hanging over him, a menace he could not elude, for he was, in some way, a prisoner of the initiative he had just taken. He couldn't leave. He had to wait for the papers presently being drawn up, otherwise his behavior would appear odd. But while he waited, they would know where he was, they could come for him, he was in the power of the police. And the worst part was that he musn't appear to be aware of all this, that he had to pretend to have a perfectly clear conscience, had to avoid betraying himself, had to seem to welcome these several days of waiting as if they were an enjoyable vacation . . .

"And when I think that I was stupid enough to say I was in no hurry."

For a second he considered going back to the ministry. But nothing is more embarrassing than changing your mind with people who have done you a favor.

"And what if I left anyway, and if I just dropped the whole thing!" he muttered suddenly.

No, on the very verge of succeeding it would really be too childish to give way to his imaginary fear. He'd never accomplish anything. Besides, he'd soon run out of money. This life had already dragged on for three months because every time an opportunity arose fear had paralyzed him. The hardest part was behind him now. He had come to Vichy. His request had been granted; all he had to do was wait.

He went back to his hotel. But upon spotting a letter in his pigeonhole he became flustered. Apart from the ministry people he had seen nobody and nobody knew he was staying here. Who could have written to him so quickly? The letter couldn't have come via the mail. Somebody had hand-delivered it. But who and why?

He took the letter. All at once he felt an immense relief. It wasn't addressed to him. The hotel owner must have placed it in the wrong pigeonhole.

"You've put in a letter that's not for me," said Bridet in an unpleasant tone.

The woman looked at the envelope. Bridet was so nervous that, for a moment, he feared she would maintain that she had made no mistake at all, that this letter was indeed intended for him. And when her apology came at last, he felt deeply relieved once more.

CHAPTER 3

On waking up the next morning Bridet suddenly had the feeling that he had been clumsy. So great was his urge to leave that not for an instant had he thought of satisfying it by roundabout means. He'd plunged straight in. The first thing he had done was to ask for a passport, a safe-conduct pass. He had stupidly shown his hand. He should have begun by contacting the people he knew, by mentioning his desire to do something useful, and by so maneuvering that he would have been told: "You ought to go to Africa, Bridet . . ." He would have let them twist his arm into going. It would not even have been he who asked for the papers himself. From the Marshal's office they'd have called Basson, "Kindly take care of Monsieur Bridet. We've given him an assignment in Rabat. It's urgent." Only then would he have called on Basson. The interview would have gone altogether differently. He would have said in a wearied tone: "They're dreadful, those friends of ours. I really would have liked enough time to make a little jaunt to Berry . . ."

While dressing Bridet pondered how his clumsiness was to be made up for. But after all, people had other things to do than keep track of his least gestures and activities. Were he to pay a call on Laveyssère today, for example, and obtain an assignment from him, when he returned to the Ministry of the Interior a week from now Basson wouldn't notice anything. Bridet would pretend he'd already had "his assignment"at the time of his first visit. Were Basson or Vauvray to appear a bit surprised, he'd say in a naive sort of way, "Oh! I thought you were in on all that."

Besides, things wouldn't get to that point. People have too many personal matters to think about. They are heedful only of the more evident features of others' actions.

He had slicked down his hair and left his worn felt hat behind at the hotel. This gave him more of the right look, for, ever since the armistice, a negligent appearance created a very bad impression, giving you something of the air of not having snapped to attention in the face of calamity, therefore of not being all that enthusiastic about the French State.

Since it was only ten o'clock Bridet strolled through the streets of Vichy. An automobile passed by. This was the third in a row with an elegant driver holding the steering wheel with just one hand, the other dangling casually outside the window. The powers that be were already solidly installed. Their foremost concern had been to war against slackness. "This is not the time," thought Bridet, "to toddle about after having had a couple of drinks."

A rotten regime had collapsed. In its stead order and cleanliness were at last arising. The soldiers who stood guard before the ministries or their ridiculous annexes wore elbow-length white gloves and the visorless headgear of the tank units. "Now we're all dolled up to look like elite troops, aren't we?" Bridet muttered as he walked past in front of them, swallowing the latter half of his sentence because he didn't know whether or not he wanted to be heard.

As he sauntered down a passageway he entered a rather fancy little novelty shop selling souvenirs of Vichy, post cards, brown wicker-encased tumblers for the medicinal waters. He asked somewhat theatrically to see the Francisques. It was to be a gift for a girl. He wanted one in colored glass if possible.

"We've never carried such an item," said the saleswoman.

"How is that possible?" Bridet exclaimed, assuming an indignant air. "I've seen them in Clermont-Ferrand, in Lyon, in Saint-Etienne. And there aren't any here, in Vichy?"

"No, Monsieur, but we have many other items. Would you care for this broach?"

"Why, what a charming idea! It's the first time I've come across that!" said Bridet, examining from every angle a broach representing the Marshal's military cap and baton with the seven stars. "Let me have two. And mightn't you have a small photograph of Pétain, something on the original side, that I could carry on me?"

"No, Monsieur. We have only the portraits you saw in the window, or else the postcards everybody is familiar with."

"What a pity," said Bridet.

Glancing at her, he caught her fighting to keep from bursting into laughter. She suddenly hurried off and another saleswoman came to replace her.

Bridet pretended not to have noticed anything, but as soon as he was outside the store he said aloud, in order that passers-by would hear: "Well, the French certainly haven't understood anything yet. The future holds some sad awakenings in store for them."

It was still a bit early to telephone Laveyssère. "Indeed

yes, you've got to have sunk pretty low to be reduced to putting on such an act," thought Bridet. He went to sit in the park at the outdoor tables of the Café de la Restauration. He recognized members of Parliament. They strolled about, arms linked. They would come to a stop, let go of one another, gesturing as they spoke, they would take hold of one another again. They did not appear to be so terribly stricken by the events. Generals passed by as well, stepping swiftly.

At ten-thirty Bridet telephoned the Hotel du Parc. It would have been quicker to go over in person but he was put off by the memory of his visit to Basson. He preferred to invite Laveyssère to lunch.

Behind the confidence placed in this man, thanks to which he had become part of the Marshal's immediate entourage, lay serious and honorable reasons that little resembled those that used to come into play before the war. No occult power stood back of the young doctor from Bordeaux. He was, naturally, neither a Free Mason nor a Jew nor a communist. He was simply the nephew of the brother of General Feutrier, himself an old military schoolmate of the Marshal from the graduating class of 1875.

They met at the Brasserie Lutétia at twelve forty-five. Unlike Basson, Laveyssère exercised no actual authority, but perhaps he held more thanks to the ready access he had to the Marshal and especially to other family connections that linked him through women to Doctor Menetrel.

After telling about what had happened to him during the retreat, an adventure he called his "odyssey," Laveyssère talked about the Paris he had returned to after the armistice to pick up his suits. What especially stuck in his mind from his trip was that the Germans had installed themselves in the finest hotels: the Ritz, the Crillon, the Claridge. He recounted how painfully he had been affected by the sight of all those Boche officers considering themselves right at home in those so elegant hotels. It was sickening. Then he spoke of a parade of German soldiers that had lasted for six hours. "And what they had in the way of equipment!"

Bridet asked if they had an arrogant air. Laveyssère considered his reply for a moment like a man who wishes to say nothing that he isn't certain of. In all sincerity he couldn't affirm that the Germans were arrogant. Actually there was something mournful about them, which you'd hardly expect in conquerors. You'd have said they were aware that the France they'd beaten wasn't the real France, our own, and that they felt a certain embarrassment in the presence of the population, it being this real France. "The truth is, I must say," continued Laveyssère, "those people don't understand why we declared war on them. They have always had a deep respect for our civilization. They fully realize that their so very rapid victory did not cause us the loss of those things through which we were their betters."

Next he related a host of little anecdotes, the gist of which was that the Germans were particularly concerned about making a good impression upon us, about showing us that they also knew how to get the best out of life. Madame James Laveyssère had got kissed in broad daylight on the Champs Elysées by a drunken soldier. An officer had intervened, and "Please believe me," went on Laveyssère, "that soldier must have paid dearly for his prank." The Germans were stern, certainly, but they had the right to be, for they were equally so toward themselves.

[25]

"Basically," said Bridet, "they aren't what we've been told."

"Oh, not at all . . ."

"I suspected as much."

"Too many people had an interest in depicting them to us as barbarians who cut little children's hands off at the wrists."

"The Jews and the Communists," said Bridet.

He felt more at ease than with Basson. Laveyssère had never shone through intelligence. The atmosphere in the restaurant, rather Parisian, rather pre-war, the fact also that Laveyssère appeared to be so very sure of what he was saying, emboldened Bridet. He thought that he ought to exploit the occasion to take a clearer stand than he had with Basson. This time he would be believed.

"Fortunately," said Bridet, "we now have men in charge who do understand. Ah! if only we'd had them before . . ."

"You're right, Bridet."

"We must get along with the Germans. I've been saying so since 1934. Personally I've always responded to them. They're people who have extraordinary qualities, you can't deny it. Like them or not like them, you simply have to admit that they have great qualities. I think moreover that today no one has any doubts about this."

Laveyssère didn't answer. Bridet, fearing for an instant that he had gone a bit far, added with a smile: "Even so, I'd prefer it if they went back home."

Laveyssère smiled also

"They too," he said with the air of a man who has his own private information, "they'd prefer to be back home."

"In that case, we'll soon come to an understanding."

Since the tone of the conversation had mellowed, Bridet thought the moment right to speak about himself.

"In the meantime, let's get down to work. The stronger

we are, the more capable we are of setting our own house in order, the more the Germans will respect us. Our empire is a first-rate asset. Personally I won't hide the fact that if I could serve our real France I'd be the happiest of men."

Since Laveyssère didn't seem to understand what Bridet was driving at, the latter had the feeling that he ought to talk a little more about the National Revolution. He was being too timid. He wasn't striking the right note. He was repeating the same mistake he'd made with Basson. Talking about the Boches was all well and good but he must also talk about the Marshal. "What keeps holding me back?" he wondered. He glanced at Laveyssère. The man was eating without appetite. You felt that the problems which were coming his way were beyond him, that he was honestly seeking to understand them. Bridet had had a little more than usual to drink. He rapped the table softly to attract Laveyssère's attention.

"We're talking too much," he said abruptly. "We should open our mouths only to shout 'Long live the new France that has just been born!' "

Laveyssère lit a cigarette. He appeared to be thinking. Then, gazing straight into Bridet's eyes, he said with a certain bitterness: "Unfortunately not everybody shares our attitude. The unhealthy forces haven't disarmed."

Bridet had the feeling that everything was going very well.

"If they still exist then what we have to do is eliminate them. France's interest before all else. I'll stop by and see you one of these mornings and I'll tell you what, in my modest sphere, I intend to do to further our safety."

"Why certainly. Come by and see me whenever you wish. Well try and set something up."

At that moment Basson entered the restaurant. He was accompanied by a gray-bearded man who fit rather well the popular image of an old-fashioned republican. In his hand he held a large black flat-brimmed felt hat. He had a slightly unkempt look which was conspicuously out of place in this restaurant. Basson walked up to the table, his companion meanwhile waiting a few steps away.

"So, still for de Gaulle?" said Basson, laughing.

Bridet reddened. Laveyssère, on the point of asking Basson whether he had replied to a certain memorandum, turned with surprise toward Bridet.

"Sure, he's a real Gaullist, one of Gaullism's hardliners, a hard-core Gaullist," continued Basson, giving his chum a friendly pat on the shoulder.

"Me?" cried Bridet.

"I'm much surprised," said Laveyssère.

"Oh, but he's a great one at camouflaging what he's up to," Basson went on, still laughing.

Bridet being visibly upset, he added: "Come now, old man, if a person can't joke anymore . . ."

Then, turning toward the man standing a few steps away: "Come over here, Rouannet, let me introduce you to one of my old friends."

"I'm very flattered," said the old-fashioned republican with a respectful bow.

"My friend Bridet is one of us. He hesitated for a little, looked around for a little to see which way the wind was blowing, but he found his course at last. Isn't that right, Bridet?"

"Now please . . ."

Addressing Rouannet, Basson continued: "You'll see him again, Rouannet. He'll be needing you."

Then, turning toward Bridet: "This is the man you'll be dealing with. Monsieur Rouannet is one of our invaluable collaborators."

"I'll be very happy if I can be useful to you," said the latter, still greatly respectful.

Then he tactfully withdrew.

A few moments later, when Bridet found himself once again with Laveyssère, he said: "Quite a guy, that Basson! Those aren't the sort of jokes to be making nowadays."

"No indeed, they're not in the best taste!" remarked Laveyssère.

"If he calls that being a Gaullist, coming to Vichy to place yourself in the Marshal's service . . . If a man like myself is a Gaullist, well, I no longer understand a damned thing—a man like me left with nothing at all thanks to that pack of Communist Jew Free Mason bastards—for they're the ones responsible, they put us where we are . . . But I certainly hope they'll be made to pay . . . and dearly. Whatever the price, they'll be getting off cheap . . . A man who was happy . . . who was leading a quiet and peaceful life, without doing any harm to anybody."

Bridet grew animated, he had finally hit the right note.

"I! I should be a Gaullist! Now that's a good one! After everything that clique did to my country . . . It's incredible that good Frenchmen didn't come forward earlier to bring them to their senses. But that's all changed now. Politics, string-pulling, scheming, that stuff's all over with."

Since Laveyssère merely nodded his head, Bridet, feigning such disgust for all those traitors that he couldn't go on talking about them anymore, abruptly shifted to a lower octave.

"I don't want to get worked up," he said.

"I don't understand," Laveyssère observed at that juncture, "why you should have taken Basson's joke so seriously."

For an instant Bridet couldn't come up with an answer. Pulling himself together: "Had somebody told you you were a Gaullist, I don't suppose you'd have been pleased about it!"

"It wouldn't have mattered to me in the least."

"Perhaps you haven't lost everything as I have."

"What do you mean? So what have you lost?"

Bridet felt a cold sweat trickling down his sides. He was marching into ever deeper water.

"I lost my country," he exclaimed, throwing out his arms.

Laveyssère looked at him as if at a stranger who had suddenly plumped himself down at his table.

"Well, now I don't understand you anymore . . ."

"Excuse me?" exclaimed Bridet forcefully, using indignation to mask his own helpless confusion.

"No, I don't understand you anymore."

"You don't understand that a man can be sickened over having been sold out, betrayed by that whole Popular Front clique, by that whole gang of scoundrels and communists!"

Laveyssère was more and more distant.

"That's something I may possibly understand," he said crisply.

"Well then, you see, you share my view!" said Bridet, taking advantage of the opportunity to moderate his tone in a natural manner.

"No, I don't share your view," continued Laveyssère, who addressed Bridet as if he had just made his acquaintance.

"Now I'm the one who doesn't understand you anymore," said Bridet.

"It's because we have entirely different ways of looking at things."

"Do you think so?"

"Yes, entirely different. We national revolutionaries weren't surprised by what happened. We foresaw the whole thing. We said it was coming time and again. We don't consider that we lost much of any importance. Therefore we don't have any cause for anger. The time for idle grumbling has passed. We don't want to go on hearing Frenchmen forever yelling about Frenchmen the way you've just done. A new France is in the process of being born. Nobody will be able to prevent it."

"And the Jews, and the communists, and the Free Masons?" Bridet tried shouting, no longer having much of an idea of what he ought to say.

"They don't exist anymore. And if they're blind to the point of not realizing what is happening, of opposing the birth of this France that comes forth in its halo of suffering, if they're blind to the point of wanting to touch this pure and glorious child, be it with the mere tips of their blood-soaked fingers, then woe betide them! They will be implacably punished. This France, whose motto is and shall be 'Work, Family, Fatherland,' has her eyes bent in our direction and if she summons us to her aid, we, the Marshal's men, will be capable of defending her, you have my word on that."

CHAPTER 4

Once he left Laveyssère, Bridet felt the need to be alone, not to see a single human face anymore. He sat down in the inner room of a café. "There's nothing to be hoped for in this town," he thought, "they're all the same. Really an awfully sorry lot. Dangerous too, because they felt themselves underrated for so long. Nobody dreamt they had such fine qualities. Impossible to discuss anything with them. They're convinced the power handed to them by the Germans was theirs by right anyway. Circumstances so combined that it fell to them in a rather unusual manner, but since it was their due, they couldn't after all be expected to refuse it."

After paying for his drink, Bridet left: "I'm not going back to the hotel. Too bad about my hat, my razor and my spare shirt. It would be just like them to be waiting for me in front of the door and then lead me off to some bureau of the police—no longer the 'judicial' police as they used to say in Paris, but the 'national' force—for everything's national now. We've never been so national. I'll simply get on the train and go back to Lyon. Once there, I'll figure out what I ought to do. What a shame my family doesn't come from Cotentin or Brittany. I would surely have found some fisherman to get me across. But Berry is where we're from and in Berry anglers are all we have by way of fishermen."

Bridet walked up Avenue de la Gare. Though still glancing from side to side in the hope of meeting with some friend who might have got him out of his difficulty, he lowered his head. He didn't want to see anybody. "And like an idiot," he thought, "by coming here I imagined I was going to find people who only pretended to be for the Boches, who would have helped me on the sly . . . that I'd find myself among fellow Frenchmen, that we'd all have supported one another."

On emerging into the large Place de la Gare, Bridet's attention was suddenly aroused. There were a lot of people. There were even some hackneys with fringed tops. But in four or five spots in front of the interminable train station façade there was also a little scene that had caught his eye. Men in pairs, empty-handed, were strolling about and scrutinizing everyone's face, and from time to time, either at random or because they didn't like a person's looks, they were stopping to question a traveler or passer-by. At first Bridet had thought that these people were acquaintances. But this scene having been repeated at different points and in an identical manner, he realized that a checking of identity papers, meant to be unobtrusive, was in progress. One of the two men examined the tendered papers, while the other was already looking about him for the next person to grab hold of. Most curious of all was that the passers-by noticed nothing at all, that life went on, that travelers were getting off a bus, that others were carrying suitcases, buying newspapers, hailing a porter.

Bridet did an about-face and walked back down the Avenue de la Gare. He turned into the first street, one which opened on his left. Vichy was a small place. Before long he would find himself on another square and perhaps observing the same incidents. This sensation of being unable to escape toward the outside, of being, no matter where he was, in a spot where someone could ask for his papers, caused him the deepest uneasiness. "And yet my papers are all perfectly in order," he thought.

He went to the post office to telephone the Hotel Carnot for a reservation. The telephones were working pretty well, considering the situation. The people at the head of the administration had been performing wonders; you felt it was a question for them of self-respect. Just because we had been beaten by the Germans it didn't mean we weren't capable of managing our day-to-day affairs. The same went for the railroads, for the collection of taxes. In short, everything was being returned to normal working order "despite the inordinately difficult conditions created by the new situation resulting from the division of France into two zones and from the presence, upon one section of its territory, of a foreign army of occupation," as the newspapers put it. The authorities, during the recent months, had pulled off some truly amazing feats. With often makeshift means they had set about repatriating several million refugees, demobilizing and putting back to work several million men. They had rebuilt bridges to ensure the distribution of foodstuffs, set up entire organizations which the Germans themselves envied us. That proved we were not the decadent country for which others were inclined to take us.

So Bridet got through to Lyon rather swiftly. Unfortunately at the Hotel Carnot, which for its part did not come within the purview of the government, there was not a single vacancy.

For an instant Bridet wondered whether he really ought

to leave at all. Would it not look odd for him to go off suddenly that way, without having let anybody know?

Bridet left the post office. The time was nearing for the train to depart. What should he do? The mere thought of returning to the hotel made it difficult for him to breathe.

It was ridiculous, but that's the way it was. That hotel, so calm, so provincial, so clean, filled him with an ever more lively fear. "Maybe I could go back and see Vauvray and that way not disturb Basson, and I could tell him I'll be spending a few days with my wife while waiting until my papers are ready." But the ministry affected him the way the hotel did. "I should have said that to Basson and Laveyssère in the restaurant. It's amazing how slow I am on the uptake."

Bridet headed mechanically toward the train station. "I'm leaving. I'll drop a line from Lyon. I'll write to the hotel, too. After all, I can perfectly well have hopped aboard a train the way you hop on a bus, all the more so since my presence here isn't required. I was told to stop by again in a week, so I'll be by in a week . . ."

As he arrived at the station Bridet first made sure that the plainclothesmen had indeed left. He bought his ticket after waiting in line for more than an hour. The platform was crowded. "This wouldn't be the moment to run into Basson a second time." At each end of the platform stood a group of policemen. Shortly they too would board the train and, proceeding along the corridors, would meet up in the middle.

Bridet arrived in Lyon at nine-fifteen, only seven minutes behind schedule. He immediately went to the hotel where his wife was living. He'd managed to get a rather decent dinner in the restaurant car.

Yolande, notified by one of the hotel's employees, was waiting for him. They sat down in the near part of the foyer.

"How did it go?" she asked.

"Very well. Not at all badly."

"Very well or not at all badly?"

"I'll let you know in a few days. My safe-conduct pass is now being drawn up. The governor needs to be telegraphed. There are a few formalities, but theoretically, I'm leaving."

"Why didn't you bring back your suitcase?"

"It was more convenient."

"Will it be there when you go back?"

"I hope so. As a matter of fact I'm going to drop a line to the hotel tomorrow."

Yolande glanced at her husband with surprise.

"You see, when I made up my mind to leave it was a sudden decision. I didn't have time to return to the hotel."

Yolande smiled.

"Yes, so I gather," she said. "You preferred to clear out as fast as possible."

"Not at all, since I'm returning to Vichy."

Two or three times they walked round the Place Carnot that lay in total darkness. They were able to make out the face of the station's illuminated clock. They talked about their separation. Then, as shadowy figures were beginning to stir about them, they returned to the hotel.

"Maybe you ought to mention that you sleep here with me," remarked Yolande. "Theoretically, that's what you're supposed to do. The police are here all the time."

"Oh, I'm beginning to get pretty tired," said Bridet, "of all these checkings of papers and verifications of identity.

They can do what they want, the police. As for me I'm going to bed, and that's the end of that."

Bridet slept badly, the bed being too small for two. At four in the morning he got up, put on his overcoat, wrapped his legs in one of his wife's coats and sat in the armchair. He was dozing when, suddenly, he heard knocking at the door of the adjoining room. It must have been daybreak for a faint glow filtered through the shutters, unless it was moonlight. He glanced at his wristwatch. It was five-twenty. Now he heard the sound of voices and commotion in the room next door. "More of these everlasting travelers," he thought. But at the same moment there were three or four consecutive knocks at his door. "Where are you?" asked Yolande, who had awoken with a start. "I'm here." "Did you do that knocking?" "No."

He switched on the light. There were more knocks. "Open up, open up," he heard. "Police."

"Police?" asked Bridet without knowing what he was saying.

"Open up. Police."

Bridet obeyed. Two men stood in the hallway. They were speaking to a third individual a few steps away who was reading a piece of paper. Other sounds could be heard off to the right, at the end of the hall. Clearly this was a police raid and right away Bridet had the reassuring feeling that they weren't after him personally. Indeed, even though he'd opened up the door, they had not as yet paid any attention to him.

"Tell the lady to get dressed," said the officer, glancing in and seeing Yolande in the bed.

"Do you have the list?" the second officer asked the one who was reading.

"In a minute," the man answered.

"What room is this?" inquired the one who had requested that Yolande get dressed, looking for the number
on the door.

"Seventy-two," said Bridet.

"I can't figure this out," said the officer. "So then we
jump from sixty-eight to seventy-two. Where are the
rooms in between?"

"At the end of the hall," said Yolande while dressing.

A fourth and fifth officer appeared, coming from that
same end of the hall.

"This hotel, you can get lost in here," said one of them.
"Is this side all done?"

"Yes, except for the fellow in sixty-four who hasn't
found his papers."

"What sort of fellow is he?"

"Foreign-looking. He must be a Jew."

"We'd have to bring him in."

Bridet went to get his wallet from his suit jacket and
took out his identity card and his discharge form.

"Here," he said to the officers who had just entered the
room.

"But what room is it?" repeated the officer without
even taking the papers.

"Seventy-two."

"Ah! okay then," said the officer, "what are you doing
here?"

"The room belongs to one person, a lady," said the
second officer while scanning the list. "Who is Madame
Bridet?"

"I am," said Yolande.

"And I'm the husband," said Bridet. "I got in from
Vichy last night. Since I didn't know where to put up I
spent the night at my wife's."

"You didn't fill out any card downstairs."

"It didn't occur to me that it was necessary," said Bridet, "since our names are the same."

"Show me your papers."

The officer examined them at length. Then calling his colleague he handed them over for the second man to examine in his turn.

"Is your name Joseph Bridet?"

"Yes."

"You got the book?" the officer asked his colleague. "Pass it to me." He spent a long time leafing through its pages, then closed it without a word.

"Are you the lady's husband?"

"Yes."

"Your identity card doesn't have a number."

"I'm quite aware of that. But it's through no fault of mine."

"And what's this discharge form here? You ever seen any certificate like this, Robert?"

"It's a discharge form. That's what we all were given after the armistice to show that we had been properly discharged, since they were so determined to do things properly."

"Did you see this form?" said the officer to his colleague. "Take a careful look."

The officer examined it at length.

"The stamp, you mean? That's a police station stamp, not an army one."

"That's quite correct. The major didn't have a stamp. He borrowed the police station's."

"No, the signature, the signature, I'm talking about the signature."

"All right, and what about it?"

"You don't notice anything, Robert?"

"No."

"It's the same handwriting. The person who filled out this certificate is the same one who signed it."

"Indeed," said Bridet. "I'm going to tell you how that happened. It's as simple as could be. By the time the armistice was declared I'd lost track of my unit and I happened to be in Ambert, in the Puy-de-Dôme, and I went over to report to the police station. They told me to wait. A few days later a major opened up an office in the subprefecture with the title of 'zone adjutant,' don't ask me where he got it. The town crier announced that all servicemen located in the city should report to him. So that's what I did. Since I was a journalist and the major lacked a secretary he grabbed me and appointed me to his staff. And that's how it was that it was I who discharged all the farmers in the district. When my turn came around I gave myself a discharge too."

"You don't have any other papers?"

"No."

The officer turned toward his colleague.

"What do we do?"

"We've got to ask the sergeant."

A few moments later, a small black-haired man whose more carefully trimmed mustache and more neatly clothed appearance revealed a higher level of authority, entered the room.

"First of all, I think you ought to know who I am," said Bridet. "My friends, Monsieur Basson at the General Headquarters of the National Police, and Monsieur Laveyssère, of the Marshal's cabinet—"

But the sergeant cut him short. "What you are doesn't make any difference. All I know is that your papers aren't in order. I'll have to ask you to come with me."

"But you don't know who my husband is," cried out Yolande.

[40]

"Please, please," Bridet said to her.

He got dressed. "In the morning I'll telephone Basson," said Yolande. Bridet made no answer. "And Laveyssère. Really, this is unheard of, a man like you being taken to the police station." After a long moment Bridet said: "I think it'd be better not to, it'll make a bad impression in Vichy. If I were in some actual danger, I would understand. But as soon as they do some investigating they'll realize that what I'm saying is the truth and they'll be forced to release me. No point alerting my friends over such a trivial matter."

Bridet looked at himself in the mirror. At that moment he was alone with Yolande. He called her over and, under his breath, he said to her: "To have to deal with such a bunch of bastards! You can be damned sure some of them will get what's coming to them one of these days." "Be still," she said to him, "you're in for trouble, I know it. I've told you already and I'm telling you again: there's only one way to get through this and that's by getting yourself in with the Boches. They're people you can talk to. They're a lot better than the French who lick their boots."

Bridet did not reply. He felt a rising anger.

"So, are you coming?" one officer bawled.

"Yes, yes, I'm coming," said Bridet.

There were about forty of them in a sort of guard room at central police headquarters. These had been installed on the premises of the main post office and took up one side of that magnificent building. There were bars on the windows, but through a sensitive afterthought on the architect's part, their lower end curved outward so as to afford room on the sill for a person's elbows or for flowerpots.

[41]

Everybody had taken a seat except for Bridet who paced back and forth. One poor woman was wringing her hands. It seemed that her daughter, a child of eight, was soon to arrive all by herself at Perrache station from Tain-l'Hermitage. She wouldn't know where to go. Bridet went up to the police sergeant who was standing near the door. "You ought to notify the captain," repeated Bridet. "I can't," answered the officer. "Well then, tell some secretary or other about it."

The policeman went out and shortly returned with a civilian clerk. "What's up?" asked the latter with the air of a man who can give you only one second of his time. Bridet recounted the poor woman's story. She had drawn near, and to Bridet kept repeating "Thank you, sir, thank you, sir . . ." The secretary left, lifting his arms in a gesture of helplessness, but without saying no.

An hour later Bridet was shown into the office of the police superintendent who already had Bridet's papers spread in front of him.

"I see you're a journalist. For which papers have you written?"

"I have been on the staff at *Le Journal* and on *Figaro*."

"*Le Journal*'s in Lyon right now, isn't it?"

"Yes, sir."

"Are you still with it?"

"No, sir."

"Why's that?"

"Because I am not interested in working under present conditions."

"Yet *Figaro* . . ."

The captain fell silent. He looked up. At that moment the two men's eyes met. Bridet's impression then was that the captain approved him.

"Do you know why you're here?" he continued.

"No," said Bridet.

"Your name didn't appear in the hotel's police register."

The captain flashed a faint smile which intimated that he himself found this reason unconvincing.

"You know how it is, the inspectors are naturally obliged to do what they're told," the captain went on. "I am too, for that matter. Here are your papers. I'm going to tell them to let you go."

"I thank you," said Bridet.

Once again the two men's eyes met. This time Bridet had no further doubt at all. He was dealing with a Frenchman. He felt a sort of secret complicity between the captain and himself.

"I thank you," he repeated.

"Oh, don't thank me! It's the obvious thing to do. We understand each other, don't we? All you have to do is go back to the waiting room. You'll be notified."

The captain rose, put out his hand rather negligently. doubtless wary of compromising himself unduly since, after all, he could be mistaken about Bridet, and while escorting him to the door, said to the two policemen who had been present during the interview: "Monsieur Bridet is going to be released shortly."

There were fewer people in the room. Bridet sat down on a bench. He had been waiting for about twenty minutes when the secretary he had spoken to a while back about that poor woman, appeared in the doorway. Pretending not to see Bridet he called: "Monsieur Bridet, please!"

Bridet got up.

"The captain has instructed me to tell you," continued the secretary, "that he has just this very instant received the order from the General Headquarters of the National

Police to release you immediately and to extend their apologies. I do so on behalf of the captain, and I inform you that you are free . . ."

A wave of warmth rose to Bridet's head. He stood dumbfounded for a moment. Finally taking hold of himself, he said: "I thank you, I thank you . . . but wouldn't it be possible for me to have a word with the captain?"

"I'm sorry," the secretary said dryly, "but the captain doesn't have time to see you."

CHAPTER 5

On leaving police headquarters Bridet headed down Rue de la Charité. Yolande had really acted clumsily. By telephoning to Vichy, by disturbing important personages–or at least those people who believed themselves such–she had certainly communicated an impression of panic. They must have imagined that something far more serious than a simple verification of identity had taken place. Yolande had got her husband into a ridiculous situation. Yet he had clearly told her to stay put. Well, she'd thought she was doing the right thing and he couldn't hold it against her.

He arrived at the hotel a little later. Formerly it had been called "Hotel de l'Angleterre." A Vichyite fanatic had found that more than he could stand, and so one night had thrown rocks at the marquee. Pieces of glass, blue-tinted because of the air raids, still lay on the ground.

Yolande had gone out. She was doubtless taking further steps in his behalf. The telephone call to Vichy had perhaps not proven effective. "It's extraordinary," Bridet thought, "how fond women are of getting themselves involved in these things."

He spotted the proprietor. He was afraid the man might reprove him, hold Bridet responsible for any subsequent problems the police threatened to cause the hotel. But no, nothing of the sort. The proprietor sent him a friendly little wave of the hand, conveying the satisfaction he felt upon seeing his guest free again. This attitude had a distinctly uplifting effect upon Bridet. It was comforting to see Frenchmen relegate their self-interest to second place behind the solidarity all men born on the same soil owe one another.

Bridet waited for more than an hour. Yolande finally reappeared. Just as he had dreaded, she had spent the morning alerting his friends. He pointed out that she would have done better had she just kept quiet. "What!" she exclaimed, "you wanted me to leave you in prison?"

Once again he felt that he and his wife stood a world apart. The defeat had left her fundamentally unchanged in her heart of hearts. She of course saw it as a catastrophe, but not of a scale that could modify a human being's normal reactions of self-defense.

She announced that she had been to see, among others, a newspaper editor. She had been very kindly received. He told her that it was out of the question that Bridet remain in prison, that he was going to attend to things.

Wringing all she possibly could out of the newspaper-man's response, she went on to say he was wrong not to have anything to do with his friends, to isolate himself as if everybody were responsible for the defeat except himself. All of the French, whatever their political opinions, were suffering as much as he. They all had to help each other.

Bridet did not reply. However, a few moments later, he said: "They all disgust me. There's nothing to be done with any of them around here. I tell you again that I want to join de Gaulle and I will join him, even if it costs me my skin."

They spent the afternoon in a packed movie theater where there was little air. Applause mingled with hooting broke out when legionnaires marched past a rostrum, in no particular formation but with upraised chins and arms outstretched. "What nobility in their gazes!" a woman shouted. "Appalling," murmured Bridet. "Keep still!" said Yolande. "Just look at that. They're giving the Hitlerian salute," Bridet said, unable to contain himself any longer. "Can't you see they're taking an oath?" an old gentleman said sharply.

They dined in a small class-D restaurant, offering a menu at twelve francs fifty. Afterwards they went for a walk along the Saône. Then, when darkness started to fall, they moved toward the hotel.

Bridet liked strolling around Place Carnot at the hour when the Germans began returning to their billets. Groups of policemen with bicycles stationed outside their hotels to see to the Germans' security occasionally poked fun at them, and coming from the authorities, this jocularity drew onlookers.

Soon, night fell. "We're going to wind up attracting attention to ourselves," said Yolande. In amidst the clumps of trees surrounding the statue of the Republic there were not only couples but also lone prowlers. These men didn't scare anybody anymore. One unexpected consequence of the defeat was that even hoodlums seemed harmless. From time to time detachments of travelers could be seen making their way down from the train station.

While passing in front of a hermetically closed window Bridet heard a radio. He stopped. Was it London or Vichy? It was London.

"Are you coming?" said Yolande.

"It's London," said Bridet.

[47]

"London's over."

"No. They're personal messages."

They heard distinctly:

"Roger's tandem is repaired."

"The chimeras are crazy."

"Albertine has never been vaccinated. We repeat: Albertine has never been vaccinated."

"The cats of the Luxembourg Garden are still meowing."

Yolande walked up.

But Bridet stayed where he was. Listening to the messages gave him pleasure. They were the indication, the only indication amid all this woe and misery, that something was happening, that somewhere in the world there still were men who fooled the Germans, who were hatching plots against them. And his confused hope was that through some undefined combination of circumstances one of the messages would be meant for him, that all of a sudden he would hear, for example: "Yolande's husband is expected in London. We repeat: Yolande's husband is expected in London."

Two days later Bridet returned to Vichy. His papers ought to be ready. Although he arrived in the morning it was only at the end of the afternoon that he made up his mind to go to the Ministry of the Interior. In these few days the carpenters and painters had given the thermal spa hotel a look more in keeping with the seriousness of the agencies now quartered there. The revolving door at the entrance hall had been taken down. The traffic in and out had become such that it had turned into an encumbrance. And perhaps security considerations had had some part in its removal. The few seconds it needed to revolve could favor some criminal getaway, an assassin's for example. The reception area had been converted into a waiting room. Partitions had been set up just about everywhere, they were covered with propaganda posters. A member of the militia wearing a helmet and a mustache and carrying a rifle stood in front of the elevator door.

Bridet felt a pang of anguish. He had the impression that something had transpired during his absence. The place was crawling with uniformed policemen. Fearing that he would be stopped and questioned if he walked by without saying anything, he asked one of them whether he knew where Monsieur Basson's office was. The officer was unable to answer. Even though he was certainly not under instructions to accompany visitors, he escorted Bridet to a table behind which sat a doorman wearing a chain the way they do in Paris and with his chest covered with medals.

The doorman consulted the register.

Seated beside him two nondescript gentlemen were conversing in low tones.

"You want to see Monsieur Basson?"

"Yes."

"Second floor."

The militiaman was still there. Bridet thanked him. This presence of an armed man at his side was deeply disagreeable to him. Some unfortunate incident must have occurred. Visitors were accompanied to keep it from happening again.

Bridet started up the stairs. On the second floor landing itself a dozen wicker armchairs stood in a row. "They must have turned the waiting room into an office," thought Bridet.

He asked for Basson. The usher came back a few moments later; Monsieur Basson wasn't in his office. Monsieur Basson was in conference with the minister, but Monsieur Basson wouldn't be long.

Bridet took a seat. On a sign he read a number of names, among them Basson's, followed by these words which exhaled an incomprehensible irritability: "Monsieur Basson receives visitors only between eleven o'clock and noon."

"They're settling in for a long stay," thought Bridet. He lit a cigarette. Between each armchair had been placed an ashtray held by a bellboy jigsawed out of plywood. Functionaries passed constantly, without a single one ever glancing at the visitors for so much as an instant.

Bridet had been waiting for an hour when four men emerged from an office. Basson was among them. Bridet half-rose in a bid for attention. He met his friend's eyes, but the latter, still all aquiver, made no sign in return.

Bridet sat back down. "As soon as he's finished," he thought, "he'll come and get me."

The four men were speaking in very audible tones, seemingly quite unafraid of being overheard. Bridet kept his eyes fastened on Basson, but Basson, as though aware of it, never glanced in his direction. "The fellow in the middle must be the minister," thought Bridet. He was a tall heavy man, dressed in an elegant suit. There was pommade on his hair. He wasn't doing any talking, nor was he doing any listening to what was being said to him. The impression you had was that the business at hand had been essentially settled and that he was lingering out of politeness only. As for the three others, there was something servile about their nervous bustling. It aimed at giving an idea ahead of time of how conscientiously and with what seriousness they would carry out their orders.

At last they parted company. The usher dashed for the stairs and, halfway down, shouted: "The minister, the minister . . ." Rifle-butts resounded on the ground floor's Second Empire mosaic tiles, then other voices: "The car, have the car pull up, the minister . . ."

In their turn the three men took leave of one another, exchanging many marks of deference, as though their boss were still present.

Once again Bridet began getting up from his seat, now convinced that Basson was going to speak to him. But the latter walked by without even turning his head.

"Basson, Basson!" called Bridet.

He didn't seem to hear. Bridet went back to the usher, rather embarrassed to have been treated that way.

"I'll go notify him that you're here," responded the usher kindly.

Bridet walked down the hallway, remaining nevertheless a few discreet steps behind.

Soon after the usher came back.

"Monsieur Basson doesn't have time to see you."

Bridet felt nearly crushed. This, then, was all that was left of their friendship, or more exactly of their long companionship from former days.

"Didn't he tell you when I could come back?"

"No, sir," answered the usher, still kindly, as if he couldn't help but find, deep down, that his new bosses were given to rather cavalier behavior. "I'll go ask," he volunteered.

He came back a little later and made a gesture of helplessness. "Monsieur Basson says you have simply to come back between eleven o'clock and noon. You'll be sure to find him in."

Bridet had scarcely stepped out into the street when the color suddenly rose to his cheeks. Not since boyhood had he blushed like this upon recalling, once alone by himself, an incident which could be considered humiliating. "The opinion they have of themselves is absolutely fantastic," he muttered. Then he chided himself for running on that way. There were millions of Frenchmen who would have been happy to go through this sort of thing for the sake of their freedom. And it wouldn't have made them blush.

The next day Bridet returned to the ministry shortly before noon, hoping that since he would be the last visitor, Basson would take him to lunch.

"Ah, you don't have any luck!" exclaimed the usher. "Monsieur Basson has just gone out. But he'll be coming back. Wait for him."

Bridet sat in the same seat as the day before. By and by he saw Vauvray go past, who appeared not to recognize him; then, the young government clerk who, a few days earlier, had asked him for his grandmother's maiden name. To kill time he picked up from a table a rather luxurious magazine which talked solely about the joys of outdoors life.

There was still no sign of Basson. At a quarter past one Bridet decided to leave. His hanging about, normal enough had his friend not been too long in returning, was becoming indiscreet.

He had just walked out the door when a car chauffeuring Basson pulled up in front of the ministry. "You don't have any luck!" the usher had said to him. It was true. A few more seconds of waiting and Bridet would have found himself face to face with Basson as naturally as could be, either in the foyer itself or on the stairs of the Hotel des Célestins. There most certainly were days when nothing happened at the moment it was supposed to. Because of those few seconds he was forced to backtrack, to wait for

Basson to get out of the car, and then to explain what had occured.

"Basson!" Bridet shouted to his friend who was walking swiftly into the ministry.

He turned around. At the sight of Bridet he showed great surprise.

"What on earth!" he said. "You show up at this hour!"

"On the contrary, I was on my way out of here, but I caught sight of your car . . ."

"I don't have the time, I don't have the time," said Basson without even holding his hand out to his friend. "Come and see me whatever day you like, between eleven and noon."

"I'll come back tomorrow," said Bridet.

CHAPTER 6

At bottom, the difficulties in getting together with Basson were a positive sign. In them Bridet saw the reassuring indication that his case had no great importance. The curiosity of the first days having passed, nobody was paying any more attention to that little business of his about a safe-conduct pass. That was all that mattered.

The next day Bridet came back more modestly at eleven o'clock. "Lunching with such people isn't exactly fun," he thought. "However only one thing counts: my papers."

This time Bridet was shown in immediately.

"So, old friend, what's been happening to you?" asked Basson.

"Nothing. I've come to see you—"

"What do you mean, 'nothing'? Didn't you just have some problems in Lyon?"

"One mustn't exaggerate . . ."

"Yet Yolande did telephone to me," continued Basson, acting like someone who couldn't quite recall just what had happened.

"Yolande?"

"Right. Yolande. I've just climbed out of my tub. At the ministry they connect me with Lyon. I say to myself,

'Now what the devil's all this?' And Yolande was on the line. Your poor wife was completely at her wits' end." Basson broke off to laugh, then he went on: "Ah! you haven't changed one little bit!"

"Yolande had a scare," Bridet stated.

"I don't see why," remarked Basson as if he didn't understand why people might be afraid of the police when they've done nothing that could be held against them.

"She imagined I was in some sort of danger . . ."

"But by the way, were you really arrested?"

"No," said Bridet. "It was just an ordinary verification of identity."

"That's not what Yolande seemed to be saying."

"Since you looked into the whole business, you know perfectly well that's all it was about."

"I know nothing at all. That's why I am asking you questions," continued Basson.

One would have said that Basson's attachment to Bridet was such that he had intervened without first seeking to inform himself and without regard for the gravity of whatever his old friend was being charged with.

"I tell you again: it was just an ordinary verification of identity."

"It didn't sound like that," Basson continued. "The police captain in Lyon simply wouldn't listen to reason. These hyper-Gaullist fellows are extraordinary! Whether you want to arrest people or let them go they're always throwing a monkey-wrench into the works."

Bridet recounted in detail what had gone on at the hotel.

"Yes, yes, I know that part. But isn't there something else?"

"Something else?" asked Bridet, suddenly worried.

"Outhenin, was he someone you knew in Paris? Do you know who I mean? At present he shuttles between the two zones . . ."

"No, no, it doesn't ring a bell."

"Well, it's not important. Outhenin spoke to me about a report. He told me they weren't happy."

" 'They' who?"

"Well, in Lyon and here too for that matter. As I told you, I'm not in the know."

"This is all beyond me," said Bridet. "A report? What about?"

"It's beyond me too."

"But you told me yourself that you straightened everything out."

"I did, but I have no idea what it's all about. I took full responsibility upon my shoulders, that's all. Come on now, tell me the truth. Isn't there a touch of Gaullism underneath all this?"

"Listen, Basson, you're being completely ridiculous. Gaullism's an obsession with you. What has that got to do with anything?"

"That's precisely what I'm asking you. Yolande telephones me. I take care of things. But there's a little bit of hesitation here, a little bit of hesitation there. Why? And this report, what's it about?"

"What report?"

"Someone told me there was a file."

"How do you expect me to know?" said Bridet.

"Look, you're not a child. They're always suspicious about something."

"I don't know anything whatsoever," said Bridet in the firm tone of a man who wants an end to further gossip.

"So this file may be imaginary?"

"You didn't ask to see it?"

"I didn't have time, and then, you understand, in your interest, it struck me that it was better not to be overly insistent. This trouble . . ."

"But there wasn't any trouble!" exclaimed Bridet who felt that he ought to display indignation but was unable to.

"Ah, as for trouble, yes, there certainly was some, all right," said Basson in a bantering tone which was in contrast with the seriousness of this revelation.

"What trouble?"

"For my part I don't know," Basson went on as if he feared that he had needlessly upset his friend.

"But I for my part do want to know," said Bridet, successfully simulating a touch of anger at last.

"I'm going to call Vauvray. You know him, I believe? He'll inform us."

"Yes, yes, I know him. But really, the fact you don't know anything is extraordinary."

A short time later Alain de Vauvray came into the office.

"Tell me, Monsieur de Vauvray, what's going on regarding our friend Bridet?"

"It's not something I know anything about," said Vauvray with a very friendly smile for Bridet. "I'm not the one who's handling the case. The report is over at Police Intelligence, I think. Outhenin's the person you should rather see."

"That's what I was saying," said Basson.

An instant's touch of dizziness caused Bridet, standing between the two men, to reel to one side. In order that it pass unnoticed he took two more sidewise steps, as though he felt like stirring his legs. He lit a cigarette but his mouth was so dry that he couldn't smoke it. Basson

picked up the telephone. Since changing offices he had at
his disposal a veritable little switchboard. He pressed one
button, then another.

"Is that you, Outhenin? Are you over on Avenue Vic-
toria? Could you perhaps run over this way? Yes, he's in
my office. He's incapable of telling me what happened.
But does a file exist or doesn't it? Yes, Bridet's here. We
ought to tidy this thing up and be done with it. Ah! So
there is a file, you say . . . I didn't know. Bring it over to
me if you can. Fine, very well, we'll be waiting for you."

Bridet, whom this conversation had made more and
more nervous, suddenly felt overcome by anger. Struggling to contain himself, he said: "You mustn't have very
much to do if you're putting together files on everybody
just for the hell of it."

Basson joked: "Files! Right now that's all we're doing,
putting together files," he said, pretending to poke fun at
himself and at the whole administration. "We have to
have archives. We can't work without archives. The
Boches are idiots. They'd do better by giving them back to
us. It would help us. Wouldn't it, Vauvray?"

Instead of answering the latter started to laugh, as people do who have no wish to compromise themselves.

Outhenin was a short, heavy-set man in his thirties, with
a low forehead and thick eyebrows. He had a slight
limp, for he had been wounded in the calf during the
"Campaign of '39-'40." One curious detail was that he
had kept the pencil-thin beard the men had worn in the
Maginot Line. Affixed to his lapel was a burnished steel
insignia upon which Bridet seemed to make out something shaped like an ax. How a man in charge of something so important as his fellow men's liberty could have
such a mediocre look strained the imagination. He was

[58]

attached to Police Intelligence. Nevertheless, for certain matters he reported to Basson. His eyes were those of an intelligent, clever, cautious man who for his superiors exhibited no more than an indispensable minimum of respect.

Basson introduced him to Bridet. Outhenin merely responded with a nod, as if this formality was liable to make him forget about the explanations he had brought. He handed Basson a blue folder upon a corner of which a machine had printed the number 864. Basson opened the folder. Bridet noticed right away that it contained nothing but a letter to which an envelope was pinned, which caused him the uneasiness we feel in connection with files that are in the course of taking shape. The addition to that letter of others was obviously foreseen.

"You call that a file!" Bridet exclaimed.

"Yes," said Outhenin.

Bridet tried reading the heading upside down but he couldn't concentrate.

"Yes, yes," said Basson while skimming the letter. "But that's his personal opinion."

Outhenin did not respond. He didn't seem to attach importance to the document he had just brought. But at the same time, through his silence, he underscored that this document did nevertheless exist.

"It's not very serious," said Basson, turning the letter at an angle so as to read a word written crosswise.

"What is it?" asked Bridet.

"Your captain in Lyon. These civil servants in the provinces are really comical!"

Then, addressing Outhenin: "Is that all?"

"Nothing else has been passed on to me," answered Outhenin. "You would have to speak to Bavardel. This sort of matter belongs in Bavardel's area."

"What sort of matter? And who is Bavardel?" asked Bridet.

"Oh, he's a really great fellow."

Turning again toward Outhenin, Basson added: "It's not worth the bother. Vauvray, nothing's come your way, isn't that right?"

"Nothing."

"Well then, we'll just wait. We'll see. Here, Outhenin, take back what's yours."

Basson rose immediately afterwards, picked up his hat and gloves.

"I have to be going."

Bridet wanted to accompany Basson. Vauvray and Outhenin had left together. But lest it be suspected that they meant to have a private discussion of this incident, they had deliberately headed in separate directions before shutting the door behind them.

"Basson," said Bridet, trying to detain his old friend, "please, stay another minute. I have to speak with you."

"I don't have time."

"You surely have a minute, come on. What's suddenly got into you?"

"I'm late . . . I'm late."

"I'll walk down with you. I do really want to know what's back of all this stuff. It's a bit much."

"I tell you I don't have the time. Besides, I don't know any more about this than you do . . . There isn't anything else I can say to you. You're deluding yourself about me. I don't run the show here."

Basson was already standing in the hallway. With his hand he beckoned his friend to come out of the office. Bridet finally advanced into the hallway. Basson pulled the door shut, then, abandoning Bridet, he moved off. He plainly did not want to walk down with his old friend. He was pretending to be in a terrible hurry. Bridet ran after him.

"And my safe-conduct pass?" he asked.

"Nothing new," said Basson, halting for a second. "The governor hasn't answered. Come back in a couple of days. I don't have the time."

He turned his back on Bridet and walked away.

So as not to follow on Basson's heels and above all to regain some countenance, Bridet went up to the usher.

"It's every day between eleven and noon that Monsieur Basson receives visitors? That's correct?"

"Yes, every day, but he's often not in."

"Oh, I see," said Bridet, who wished to prolong the conversation. "I imagined that in as much as its says . . ."

The usher smiled.

"You know, these gentlemen are so burdened with work . . ."

Bridet was about to leave when the door to Room 12 opened. A man appeared. It was Rouannet.

"Ah, Monsieur Bridet," he exclaimed, "you're the very person I wanted to see. Could you wait for me a moment? I'll be right back."

Bridet started pacing up and down the foyer. All round him he sensed a confused milling activity. Pieces of paper concerning him were circulating from office to office. How was it they told him nothing? It was more and more disturbing. Basson's attitude was peculiar. He had been cordial, then, suddenly, he had changed. And that report? A report by whom and about what? But, just before, hadn't Rouannet spoken to him very kindly? "In reality, nothing's going on. It's on account of Yolande's blunder in telephoning. It's always the same," he thought, remembering Rouannet, "strangers are more straightforward and nicer than our friends."

Rouannet reappeared a little later. He was still as considerate as at the restaurant. He gave the impression that, through lack of psychological acumen, he supposed Bridet belonged to the somewhat malevolent and embittered social class which had just assumed power, and which, though still barred from certain jobs by the old guard, was making it plain that it was aware of its strength.

"Please take a seat, Monsieur Bridet," said Rouannet, pushing forward an armchair and going to great lengths to appear amiable.

Bridet was surprised that Rouannet occupied such a large office and that the employees under him showed him the same deference he himself showed all the young civil servants.

"I was about to write you," said Rouannet.

Bridet remarked that he had a far clearer grasp of his role than had the various Outhenins, Bassons and Vauvrays. He didn't look as if he believed all this had just come about out of the blue, as they say. He never once telephoned to any service at all.

"Wait," he said, after a genuine search for a piece of paper.

He opened a door, called to a secretary. As she did not appear right away, he walked into the adjoining room.

"So sorry," he said on his return.

He had left the door open.

"Bring me Monsieur Bridet's safe-conduct pass," he called out, nobody having come.

At last he sat down.

"I meant to write you," he continued, "to tell you your

papers are ready. We received a reply to our telegram the day before yesterday. The governor naturally raises no objection to your coming to Africa. By the way I ought to tell you that our request was made simply out of courtesy toward him. He cannot do otherwise than defer to it. But before getting your safe-conduct pass typed up I wanted to ask you if you would not prefer that it be marked 'round trip.' It strikes me as wiser. In the event you didn't like it over there you wouldn't need to apply for anything in order to come back. Africa's very nice, but believe me, before going there it's better to make sure you'll be able to leave again."

"You're right," said Bridet.

"Perfect. I shall therefore have your safe-conduct pass drawn up for a six-month period. That's what we usually do. And I'll submit it for signature this afternoon."

"Who has to sign?" asked Bridet, suddenly afraid that it might be Basson.

"The chief private secretary of the Director General, Monsieur Reynier."

"Oh, fine, that's very good . . ."

Bridet had just had the feeling that his luck was turning. During that earlier visit, when he had seen Basson, the latter had doubtless not been aware that the governor's answer had come. Basson had simply said the first thing that came into his head, in order to be rid of his friend. Besides, these formalities were no longer his department. Bridet was doing nothing wrong by appearing to forget what Basson had told him. He certainly wasn't about to prevent Rouannet from drawing up his safe-conduct pass. Since this official considered that he could give it to him, Bridet wasn't going to tell him, "Yes, but what about this, what about that . . ."

"All you have to do is come back tomorrow," said Rouannet. "Unless you'd prefer that we have it brought to your hotel."

"I'd prefer to come back," said Bridet.

On leaving the ministry Bridet felt uneasy nonetheless. "I acted foolishly. I should never have brought up my papers again with Basson. He had accepted. Now I look as if I'm proceeding secretly, disregarding him altogether."

Bridet went to lunch. He was still preoccupied. This signature business especially concerned him. Was this Monsieur Reynier just going to sign like that, without any looking into the matter, simply because the document was put in front of him? Had Basson mentioned Bridet to him? Wasn't this Monsieur Reynier going to jump to his feet, to go and find Basson and tell him: "But I thought you were against giving him a safe-conduct pass?"

"If Basson says anything to me," thought Bridet, "my answer's simple: 'You ran off so fast . . . I didn't understand what you told me . . . When Rouannet called me in I thought you knew what was going on, that it was you yourself who had settled it all with Rouannet. You can't expect me to have been better informed than the people in your own department."

But try as he did to reassure himself, Bridet's conscience bothered him. There was no getting around it, in his behavior there was something equivocal. He thought about it during the entire meal, then, sitting on the terrace outside a café, towards three o'clock, tired of thinking about the whole thing, a vast dislike for Vichy suddenly took possession of him. All he had to do was pick up and leave immediately. Never again would he set foot in this abominable town. There was nothing to be got from such people. They kept him dancing attendance. They were trying to put him in a grotesque position. It was even possible the whole thing was a deliberate fabrication. Rouannet, Reynier, Basson were working hand in hand. They were about to call him in for the comedy's big scene: "What, you did such a thing as that! Why, you don't understand the serious implications of your actions!" It was best to leave immediately. They could keep it, that safe-conduct pass of theirs.

This moment of anger once past, Bridet came to the decision that to him seemed the simplest. Whatever might happen, he would leave Vichy the following day, but before leaving he would go one last time to the ministry. He would ask for Rouannet. If the latter was evasive, if the safe-conduct pass wasn't signed, Bridet would make as if he was not surprised. He would say, so as not to arouse suspicion, that he would be back in the afternoon, the next day, but at once, without hesitation or regret, he would proceed on foot to Cusset. There he would take a bus for Saint-Germain-des-Fossés, where he would board the first train to Lyon. This way he would not have to contend with the surveillance at the Vichy railroad station.

This course of action once laid out, he thought that while waiting he should not neglect to do whatever might consolidate his position vis-à-vis the police officials. Instead of roaming about the streets he would go and visit Laveyssère right away. He would not ask him about anything. He would talk to him about this and that, would give him to understand that he was getting the hang of things in Vichy, was even getting to like the place, that he was in no hurry at all to be off. Notwithstanding that he would make an occasional discrete hint at an eventual departure. He might perhaps be going to Africa. As a matter of fact they were taking care of him over at the Ministry of the Interior. A safe-conduct pass was now being got together for him. A wire had gone off to the governor of Algeria. He didn't know whether there had been an answer. Basson hadn't received anything. But, on the other hand, in the departments they seemed to think an answer had arrived. He planned to spend the next day at the Hotel des Célestins, he wanted to have the whole thing clear in his own mind. Basically though he didn't have much of an urge to leave anymore. When he'd come to Vichy it had been in the belief that he could best serve France in her Empire. But since then he had talked to a lot of people and now his feeling was that he would be still more useful were he to stay.

When he got to the Hotel du Parc he stood there, not daring to enter. It was sheer madness, but he was afraid lest all these military, private, plainclothes and municipal policemen who were standing guard at the entrance, coming and going through the foyer and constantly conferring, might, instead of simply directing him to Laveyssère's office, subject him to an interrogation out of which he wasn't sure he could come with flying colors.

He went for a stroll under the interminable marquee covering the macadamized lane bordering Boulevard Albert 1er. No, he most certainly wasn't big enough to take on all these people.

CHAPTER 7

Bridet was up early the next day. He had decided to pay his bill and to leave his suitcase at a small café next to the bus station. Only after doing that would he go over to the ministry. That way he would feel more free. No matter what he would leave that same day, with or without papers.

There was nobody in the office of the Hotel des Deux-Sources. He knocked at the windowed door, then opened it, hoping the sound would attract somebody. He put his suitcase on the cane settee in the entry, then walked down the long corridor opposite the stairway. At the end of this corridor there was a door that connected with an adjoining café. Bridet had often wondered if the two establishments, hotel and café, belonged to the same owner, considering how different the two sets of clientele were. He opened the door halfway. On the counter stood toasted slices of cheap bread in place of croissants.

"Is the lady from the hotel here?" asked Bridet. "I'm giving up my room and I'd like to settle my bill."

"Isn't she in her office?"

"No."

"Wait. I'll go and see."

A big woman wearing a white apron went off to look for the owner.

"She must be in her room," she said, after having opened two or three doors.

Bridet waited in front of the office. Nobody had yet left for the day, since there were no keys hanging at any of the pigeonhole hooks. Bridet rubbed his hands together. It was a way he had after washing up in the morning. Ever since awaking he had been wondering what the most suitable time would be to drop in on Rouannet. Nine-thirty was hurrying it a bit, although they would have you think they were early risers in Vichy. Ten o'clock, yes, ten o'clock, that would be about right. Or a quarter after ten. But Basson was liable to have arrived before then. "I ought to have asked the usher about that yesterday when I was hunting for something to say to him anyway."

At that moment he saw the big woman in the white apron coming back from the second floor.

"Madame will be down," she said.

An instant later the hotel owner appeared. She was a blonde woman, but already along in years. She had on a gaudily colored peignoir. Nevertheless she gave an impression of utmost respectability. "She's already prepared my bill," thought Bridet, noting the envelope in her hand. "She did it fast."

"Are you leaving, Monsieur?" she asked, holding out this envelope to Bridet.

"Yes."

"Very well. I'll go and prepare your bill."

"This isn't the bill?" asked Bridet, showing the envelope.

"No, no. It's a letter that was brought for you this morning."

Bridet felt his pulse quicken.

"Why didn't you put it in my pigeonhole?"

"I was asked to deliver it to you in person."

Bridet tore open the envelope, but he was trembling so much that he tore what was inside at the same time. Fitting the two pieces together, he read:

French State.

National Security.

Office of the Director.

H.C. 17.864.

Vichy, October 13, 1940.

M. Joseph Bridet is requested to stop at the National Security offices, 18 Rue Lucas, on Thursday morning at 10 AM, for a matter concerning him personally.

For the Director General.

Written over something stamped in red was a snakelike mark representing a signature. Diagonally and underlined, the word "Summons" had been written out in ink.

"Here's your bill," said the owner.

Bridet cast a startled glance at the printed form, of the usual long and narrow shape, that was being held out to him. During the time he had spent reading the summons the owner had sat down at her desk, looked for a pen, uncorked a bottle of ink, consulted her ledgers, listed the supplementary charges, added up all the numbers on a piece of scrap paper alongside, and recopied the sum total onto the bill. Then she had got up and brought it over to him. She had done all those things without his even noticing.

Bridet paid and left. Gray clouds, blending into each other, hid the sky. It was eight-thirty. Few people were abroad. You'd have thought there'd been some festivity the night before. A jumble of empty chairs still stood around the bandstand. A few isolated ones stood at the foot of trees, some others lay tipped over on the ground, some, collected in groups of five or six, or in pairs, suggested circles of elderly ladies or couples in love. Bridet heard singing. A squad of uniformed but unarmed youths passed by, their heads held high, proud frowns upon their faces. The word "hope" recurred endlessly upon their lips.

For some minutes Bridet walked straight ahead, thinking of nothing, as if nothing had happened, walked along just as normally as could be, guided by that instinctive reaction which, when we are confronted with pain or calamity, causes us to hide our emotion for as long as we possibly can.

Then he stopped, re-read the summons. "That does it . . ." he murmured. He went over the events of the preceding day. "That's it. They are going to say that I tried to obtain my papers by fraud. They are going to arrest me. Now they've got their grounds for doing so. Oh, I sensed it was something I shouldn't be doing. How could I have imagined for one second that I was going to pull one over on them? They must be furious! That sly devil Rouannet is the one behind this. It must have been done with Basson's connivance. This whole thing, it was set up between them, and like some imbecile I fell right into the trap."

Once again Bridet came upon the squad he had already encountered, at whose head marched an officer who never once turned to look at his men, so sure was he of their perfect performance.

At that moment the feeling came to Bridet that there was nothing he could be reproached for. His defense was easy. He had acted sincerely. He had not believed he was doing anything wrong. He would tell them at National Security that as a matter of fact he intended to go and see

Monsieur Basson. The name would make its nice little impact. He would say that Monsieur Rouannet was the one who had called him, who had first spoken to him about his safe-conduct pass. Not for one instant could he have imagined that Monsieur Rouannet was exceeding his powers. He would say: "I didn't know. You couldn't expect me to have been wary of a public official."

After noting that he was not being followed, Bridet told himself that after all he was still free. He could very well have not received this summons, and so not answer it. Indeed, if on leaving he hadn't asked to see the hotel owner she wouldn't have been able to put it in his hands. Nothing still prevented him from leaving. He could very well catch the first bus for Saint-Germain-des-Fossés, disappear.

While he went on walking his confidence returned. What proved that this "matter concerning him personally" entailed danger for him? On the contrary, this was perhaps a felicitous event. They had decided to give him an appointment overseas. They simply wanted to get a piece of information from him. There was nothing anywhere against him, nothing in writing, nothing tangible. Besides, there wasn't anything he had done. He had said, some time ago, to a fair number of people, that he was looking to join de Gaulle, but if you were going to have to arrest everybody who had said the same thing . . . On the other hand, since being here, he had said plenty of times how much he admired the Marshal. He had even perhaps gone a bit overboard the day he told Laveyssère that he venerated him.

Even supposing that certain persons had been informed of remarks he had made elsewhere, there was no reason to give those remarks any greater credence than those he was uttering at present. Against him the only negative thing they could do was assume a distrustful attitude, back away from him. Actually, they were perhaps calling him in to notify him that they weren't able to give him a safe-conduct pass. They were going to tell him that, upon further consideration, his departure was deemed inopportune. This word "inopportune" was much in use at the moment. There was a polite firmness to it which the Vichyite authorities liked enormously.

CHAPTER 8

At ten o'clock sharp Bridet arrived at Rue Lucas. He had given up the idea of depositing his suitcase at a café near the bus station, fearing that, if he was being followed, it might be supposed that he didn't intend to respond to the summons. He placed it in safekeeping with a shop owner who moreover raised a fuss before agreeing to look after it.

Rue Lucas, very close to the city park, was as calm and quiet as could be. The street was without a single store. Rather, you saw handsome plaques with the names of physicians at the entrance to nearly every building. Bridet had considerable trouble locating the National Security office. There was no sign that could be seen from the street. Nor was there anything under the archway. He opened a windowed door into a vast foyer in the center of which rose the main staircase. Upon a cardboard sign hanging from the decorative brass ball surmounting the newel post were written the two words "National Security." There was no mention of what floor.

Since there didn't seem to be a concierge, Bridet went back outside, knocked at a window in the courtyard. "Typical of the bureaucratic mentality," he thought. "These gentlemen imagine they're indispensable. Can't possibly do without them, right? You want to see them, well then you can just take the trouble to look for them. It's not for them to worry about where they are to be found."

National Security was installed in space on the mezzanine. Only the office hours were indicated on the door. Bridet rang. It was silly, but it bothered him that there was nothing on the door inviting you to enter without knocking. Nobody answered. He turned the knob and found himself in a vestibule furnished with a cheap wood table and a chair reserved for an employee. The employee was absent. Bridet read the word "Information." He knocked at a door.

"Come in," somebody shouted.

He stood in the presence of four men, each seated at a small individual desk. He got the feeling that he had interrupted a conversation. These men examined him. Bridet went up to the one nearest the door and showed him the summons. The clerk probably read it over several times, for he remained quite some time staring at those few lines.

"You're Monsieur Bridet?" he asked at last.

"Yes, that's who I am."

"Monsieur Joseph Bridet?"

"Yes, yes."

The clerk turned toward his colleagues, visibly sorry that he found no other questions to ask.

"Our boss isn't in yet, is he?"

For a moment Bridet thought he could take advantage of this in order to leave. He said: "In that case will you be so kind as to say I was here and will be by again later."

The four men glanced at one other.

"If you've been summoned, it's better for you to wait," said one of them.

"I was summoned for ten o'clock."

"Sure, I know, the Director will be here shortly," said another, trying to come across as having been around longer than his colleagues.

"All right," said Bridet. "Fine."

"Just take a seat in the entrance hall. He's always here ordinarily. He's late."

Bridet sat on a polished oak bench set against the wall. An unshaded bulb lit the vestibule. A little light also entered through a frosted glass door, probably the door to the former kitchen. There was no carpeting, but some brass tacks remained driven into the wooden floor. On a wall, somewhat off center and a bit out of the light, hung a small photograph of General Weygand. He was in uniform, bare-headed, which gave him the air of an independent man, ready to pursue whatever struck him as the best course at the opportune moment.

Every now and then the entrance door would open. Nobody seemed to notice Bridet's presence. The visitors walked on down the hallway unhesitatingly, opened doors to look in, shut them again.

Bridet felt less worried. He told himself that in the event of something truly serious the director wouldn't have been late. His being in so little hurry to see Bridet indicated that he had more important matters to attend to. Bridet lit a cigarette. He noticed that the lock hardware had been removed, no doubt by the previous tenants, leaving holes in the door the size of a two-franc coin. There was something warming about this detail. You had the feeling they were in here on a temporary basis. They didn't seem to be focussed on arresting people.

After a half-hour's wait Bridet got up and started pacing back and forth in the vestibule. By now the visitors he had seen entering had gone back out. Some had even returned.

It was becoming embarrassing to still be there. Moreover, it could be that the Director had arrived and they had forgotten to tell Bridet.

He knocked softly at the door of the room occupied by the four clerks.

"If he was here," they said, "we'd know it."

Bridet went back to his seat in the entrance. He thought he'd simply leave a written message, say that he had come, had waited, but since he had an engagement, had been obliged to leave.

At that moment an elegant young man, coming from some inner office, stopped in front of him.

"Are you Monsieur Bridet?" he asked.

"Yes."

"Monsieur Saussier is sorry about being late. He'll be here in fifteen minutes at the very most. He requests that you wait for him."

"This is really very awkward," said Bridet, comforted by this courteous tone. "The fact is, I'm supposed to be seeing Monsieur Basson in a little while, at the Ministry of the Interior. Is it eleven o'clock?"

The young man glanced at his watch.

"It's not yet eleven," he said.

"Yes, but it'll take me some time to get there."

"Do you want me to telephone Monsieur Basson to tell him you're here?"

"Oh, no! It's not worth the bother."

"Do you want to make the call yourself?"

Bridet pretended to find that an excellent idea, then suddenly, as if changing his mind: "Oh, after all, he'll wait for me."

Bridet sat back down. Another half-hour went by, punctuated by an ever-growing number of comings and goings. Now and then the elegant young man came back to keep up the visitor's patience. Finally, as if wondering that the idea hadn't occurred to him earlier:

"But why not come into my office? You'll be much more comfortable. Forgive me for not thinking of it before."

"You know, it's already eleven-thirty," remarked Bridet.

"If you're worried on Monsieur Basson's account, put your mind at rest. I just telephoned to Interior. He won't be coming in this morning."

"Well, in that case, fine, that changes everything," said Bridet, appearing relieved. "I can wait."

At the far end of the corridor there was a nook where a dismantled dining room sideboard and a set of bed-springs were being stored. The secretary opened another door. Much to Bridet's surprise it revealed a small inner staircase, newly constructed.

"I'm having you take the short cut," said the secretary. "Excuse me, I'll precede you to show you the way."

"But where are we going?" asked Bridet.

"Upstairs."

An instant later Bridet was standing in another suite which had nothing in common with the one he had just left. It was luxuriously furnished. From the foyer, to which a red carpet, three-branched lighting fixtures on the walls and a kind of sideboard with gilded feet provided a high tone, there could be made out, through windowed double doors, an equally sumptuous salon.

"I'll go and inform our director," said the secretary. "He must have arrived now."

To this Bridet's response was something like a silent hiccup. What was the meaning of this elegant young man's odd attitude? Why was he now saying that the Director was there, when he had simply come to get the visitor in order to show him to a more comfortable place? Bridet didn't have time to ponder it further. The secretary parted the doubled doors.

"May Monsieur Bridet step inside?" he inquired.

From within came the reply: "Why, of course."

The secretary disappeared and Bridet suddenly found himself in the large room, brightly lit, cheerful. On his left he perceived, at the far end, a man seated behind a desk that could not be seen from the foyer. This man got up. His very sparse hair lay flat, as if painted on the crown of his head. He wore a starched collar and, on his lapel, a Legion of Honor rosette whose bright red stood out against the dark color of his suit. Bridet sensed at once that, unlike what had been the case heretofore, he was no longer dealing with friends of his own generation or younger men taking on enigmatic airs so as to impress, but was now facing a genuine high official. This Monsieur Saussier was clearly somebody. He owed nothing to the defeat. He must have already held other important posts before the war.

"I'm sorry," said Monsieur Saussier, "for having kept you waiting. Do please sit down. I asked you to come by this morning because I need to speak with you."

"Indeed, Monsieur, yes, it really doesn't matter, it's altogether natural."

"You are, I believe, a great friend of our exceedingly likeable Basson."

"Not a great friend. I'm simply a friend of Basson," Bridet answered prudently.

"But you were happy to run into him again, were you not?"

"Most happy," said Bridet.

"Did you know he was here?"

"I found out in Lyon."

"How?" asked Monsieur Saussier casually.

One sensed that he found it rather irksome that he, given his importance, be obliged to ask such seemingly innocuous questions. Furthermore, the while doing so he kept jotting notes on papers, as if, busy with other things, he continued speaking merely to keep the conversation alive.

"In the simplest way in the world. During the weeks following the armistice we all tried to find out not only what had become of our friends but sometimes even of people who were of no particular importance in our lives."

"Yes, yes, I went through the same experience. What memories!"

"It isn't just him I've been to see, let me add. I've also been to see Laveyssère, whom you no doubt know. He is in the Marshal's cabinet. He's one of my friends, or rather a friend of my wife's family. James Laveyssère's mother's maiden name is Quatrefage. My father-in-law was for a long time the director of FLA, the France-Latin America shipping company, one of whose founders was Monsieur Laveyssère senior."

"Yes, yes, but I'm afraid we are straying. Let's get back to Basson. You had asked him, according to what I was told, to help you leave—that's right, isn't it?"

"Not exactly. I said to him: 'I've come to place myself in the Marshal's service.' My zeal caused him to smile just a little. He said to me: 'That's very fine on your part, but do you have something in mind?' Then my thoughts turned to our empire. I told him: 'You ought to send dependable men out there.' "

"And what was Basson's reaction to that?"

"He approved. He said moreover that that's what they were doing and he'd send me out as soon as he could. I believe furthermore that it's been taken care of. Actually,

I was supposed to go by the Ministry of the Interior this morning. I won't claim that it's so, but it would seem that my papers are ready."

Monsieur Saussier looked as if he were delighted by this news.

"Really," he said, "Basson has been very nice to you."

"Very."

Saussier pressed a button. A man appeared in the doorway, not as a secretary would have appeared, but with the familiarity of a relative or a friend.

"Come on in, Schlessinger."

He was a tall, slender man, stoop-shouldered and with a long, finely-modeled and arched nose. He carried a gold lorgnette. By allowing cigarette ash to fall upon his person he strove for an effect of inattention, such as is found in the elderly. It was harder to make out what his origins were than with those others, with Outhenin, Basson, Vauvray, Rouannet or even Saussier. He gave the impression of an academic having no personal involvement in politics but who had known how to make himself indispensable in circles that did. He had perhaps thought that his prolonged studies would lend him greater distinction in a place where they weren't necessary. He had perhaps renounced the goal for whose sake he had originally pursued them and sacrificed a youthful ideal in exchange for more rapidly come by prestige and material advantages.

Bridet smiled. In reality he was in an extraordinarily overwrought state. He didn't have a clue as to what was going on. He didn't see why he had been summoned. They seemed to want to exchange a few ideas with him. But honestly now, you don't summon people to police headquarters to exchange ideas . . .

Monsieur Saussier addressed his collaborator.

"I would like to repeat to you what Monsieur Bridet has just told me, it's very interesting."

"Is that so? Well then just wait a moment," said Schlessinger. "I'm going to get my briefcase."

Bridet gazed in amazement at the Director of National Security. Whatever had he said that was so interesting?

Schlessinger came back in a few moments. He sat down by the desk, pushed some papers aside, placed his briefcase in front of him.

"Sit in my chair," said Saussier, "you'll be more comfortable."

"Oh, thank you, this is fine," answered Schlessinger, glancing at his wristwatch. "You know, it's half-past twelve. We might do better to start this afternoon."

"I'll only be a minute or two. It's preferable that you hear this. We'll continue this afternoon if necessary. I am going to give you a quick summary of Monsieur Bridet's statements."

"Statements!" exclaimed Bridet, laughing. "That sounds a bit formal . . ."

"Here we are," continued Saussier, not appearing to have heard this interruption. "Monsieur Bridet claims that, desiring to serve our government, he came to Vichy on his own, without anyone's invitation, in order to contact his friends. He saw Basson, Monsieur Laveyssère. Is that correct, Monsieur Bridet?"

"Yes it is. Or almost correct, for this isn't *claiming* on my part, it's the truth."

"It doesn't tally exactly with what Basson told me," observed Schlessinger who had not yet opened his briefcase.

"Do you believe then that it would have been Basson who took the initial step?" Saussier went on.

These last three words, "the initial step," sent a chill through Bridet. Schlessinger turned toward him at that moment. He had a cigarette in his mouth. The smoke made him blink.

"Will you positively state that you never saw Basson anywhere else than in Vichy—never in Lyon, for example?"

"Never," declared Bridet who just then, for the first time, had the impression that all this had to do not with him but with Basson. The latter had done something serious. Unable to answer for his actions before his colleagues, the investigation was being conducted by someone outside the police, yet with connections to it.

His vision blurred, as if a liquid come from somewhere else had overspread his eyes. If Basson were guilty of something, he, Bridet, by exaggerating their friendship and even using it as a reference, had admitted partnership in that guilt.

Schlessinger opened his briefcase. He drew out a few papers which he passed to Saussier, who read them attentively.

"Vauvray and Keruel may have been misled by Police Intelligence," remarked Saussier a little later.

"Why?"

"I thought that no carbon existed."

"Oh yes there does, Hild isn't so stupid. He knows those people."

For the past minute Bridet had been hunting for some way to retract what he had said, some way to rid his friendship for Basson of the importance he had imprudently lent to it. He was perspiring so much that the sweat was reaching his collar and dampening its edge. He had lost not a word in the exchange between the two policemen, but such men were masters in the use of covert language to communicate with one another in the presence of a third party.

"You intrigue me, gentlemen," he said, striving for a natural air. "What's all this about then?"

"Basson maintained that he did indeed know you, that you had come by to pester him, but that each time he had shown you the door, and never for one second had any thought of giving you a safe-conduct pass for Africa. He even said in so many words that you inspired no confidence in him at all."

"What's that?" cried Bridet, simulating indignation. "Do you want me to telephone him in front of you?"

The two police chiefs exchanged signs.

"He doesn't have a phone anymore," Monsieur Saussier could not keep himself from interjecting.

"Try and stop by the Hotel du Parc after lunch," said Schlessinger. "De la Chazelle has got to let us have the telegrams, at least until this evening."

Bridet rose halfway to his feet.

"I insist on telephoning," he repeated.

"Take it easy, Monsieur Bridet."

"I've been here for three hours. If this is the way you treat people who wish to serve the Marshal—"

"Now be careful what you say, Monsieur Bridet."

"The Marshal is certainly not aware of what's going on around him. He wouldn't tolerate it if he knew."

Saussier and Schlessinger glanced at each other.

"You're starting to push your luck," observed the Director of National Security. "Leave the Marshal in peace."

"We'll resume our conversation," said Schlessinger, looking at his watch. "It's already one-twenty."

Addressing Bridet, but in a much less cordial tone than at the start, as though he had recovered his liberty thanks to Bridet's fit of temper, Saussier went on: "I fear that you'll not find any of the restaurants still serving. So take the stairs down to the floor below. One of the gentlemen you saw on your arrival will show you to a very good friendly little restaurant that's nearby. That way you'll be able to return here right after lunch so that we can wrap this business up."

Bridet nearly said that he had an appointment else-where, but he was so afraid of discovering that he was a prisoner that he preferred that things stay nebulous.

"Why, that's a splendid idea!" he said.

CHAPTER 9

Bridet had lunch with an inspector by the name of Bourgoing who, for the benefit of customers and waiters,
strove, rather clumsily, to have it look as if he had got
back together with an old chum whom he was absolutely
bent on staking to a good time. After the meal Bourgoing
ordered liqueurs, giving one the feeling that in circumstances like these his superiors did not too closely scru-
tinize his expense account receipts.

At three-thirty they returned to Rue Lucas. Along the
way Bridet was seized by a little impulse to independent
action. Without forewarning his companion he ducked
into a tobacco shop. The inspector was about to follow
him, but changing his mind, waited for him outside.

They went straight up to the second floor by way of the
main staircase, but instead of being led, as he expected,
directly to Monsieur Saussier's office, Bridet was shown
into a small room upon the door of which was affixed the
calling card of a certain Yves de Keruel de Mermor.

There were no hothouse carnations on this desk as
there had been on Basson's, but instead, between two
glass squares in a nickel-plated stand, a large photograph
showing a very pretty woman with each arm around a
child of ten or so. The pose recalled the one in a portrait

by Madame Vigée le Brun. Such was the perfection of this evocation of Monsieur de Keruel de Mermor's private life that there was nothing of familial feeling about it, giving rise in the mind of the beholder to the suspicion that the picture had merely come from some expensive magazine.

The wait was becoming unbearable. As the afternoon wore on, Bridet had the ever sharper impression that he was not to recover his freedom, that there wasn't going to be time enough left, in Saussier's words, to wrap his business up. Therefore they'd hold him in custody. Since he hadn't been allowed to eat lunch alone, there was no reason why they should allow him to have dinner or spend the night alone. From time to time Bourgoing would arrive with the request that he be patient for a little longer. Monsieur Saussier was going to be here any moment, he would say, and yet, when the door stood open, Bridet would hear the director's voice.

At five o'clock Keruel himself entered the room. With him, for no apparent reason, was Bourgoing. He was a tall bony-faced man with a prominent Adam's apple, and he was smartly got up in a gray flannel suit and a white foulard with blue polka dots. Until now all the functionaries Bridet had come in contact with had affected to show much consideration for him. This was no longer so. Keruel didn't utter a word.

"Am I disturbing you?" asked Bridet who still insisted, albeit very weakly, on preserving the appearance of an ordinary visitor.

"Not in the least," responded Keruel shortly.

He sat down at his desk, then without looking at Bridet: "Monsieur Saussier has instructed me to see you . . ."

These words froze Bridet. Nothing was harder for him to put up with than this continually having to deal with someone new. It was dreadful. Once he thought he had gained the sympathy of one, he would find that he had to start all over again with another. Bridet turned around instinctively in the hope of seeing the inspector. It made no sense at all, but his presence would have been a comfort.

Keruel had taken a bunch of keys from his pocket. He opened the drawers of his desk, then, picking up the telephone, he spoke a long while without showing any interest in Bridet. He took his new duties so very seriously that he had mixed all his keys together—the old set, to his property in Brittany, and those for Vichy. When he ended his conversation he started writing. A half-hour went by this way. Keruel had still not addressed one word to Bridet when the door opened. It was Monsieur Saussier.

"Will you step into my chambers," he said without appearing to recognize Bridet. "You come as well," he added, speaking to Keruel.

A few instants later Bridet found himself in the same large office he had been in that morning. But it was no longer the elegant and quiet room where a bureau chief makes his decisions and an outsider enters only with circumspection. All its doors stood wide open; there was tobacco smoke in the air. Monsieur Schlessinger sat in the director's chair; his briefcase lay before him on the desk. Two men were in conversation near a window; a third was seated in an armchair. The sound of a typewriter came from a neighboring room.

Bridet halted, as if he felt he was intruding. "Come in," Saussier said to him, "come in, come in."

The thought that all these people had foregathered on his account threw Bridet into a momentary panic, but he saw that nobody attached any importance to his person. The doors remained open. He regained confidence.

"Sit down," said Saussier.

Bridet obeyed. He looked at Schlessinger, then at the three unknown men. No, none of them seemed concerned about him at all. But then suddenly his eyes met the eyes of one of the men. A wave of heat rose to his head. Those eyes had immediately shifted elsewhere as if their look had been detected.

A few minutes went by during which Bridet, listening to what was being said, tried to understand the reason behind this meeting. But the conversation bore upon the Ministry of Finance. It seemed to have been very clever on the Marshal's part to have yielded to the Germans' desire to see it re-established in Paris. This made for a foothold in the capital. In a few weeks another ministry would follow. And one fine day, without realizing how it had happened, the Germans would find themselves looking at a French government solidly implanted in Paris.

One of the two men over by the window came towards Bridet.

"A cigarette, Monsieur Bridet?" he said, pressing the button on his case.

"With pleasure," said Bridet, frightened again by the fact that this unknown person had addressed him by name.

"We're costing you a lot of your time . . ."

"It wouldn't matter," Bridet rejoined, "if I knew why. But nothing's more worse than waiting around like this, for hours on end . . . You pretty much get the impression that these days . . ."

Bridet broke off, not daring to bare his thoughts.

"Oh," said the man, smiling, "you mustn't let yourself get worked up. Events warrant these changes in standard practice. We must no longer be surprised by anything. Nothing's ruled out these days."

Bridet felt that his interlocutor, although he'd not ceased smiling, was finding a sort of vicious satisfaction in speaking to him this way. The easygoing days with their considerate and gracious behavior were over now. It was rather as if he, Bridet, had not grasped the underlying meaning of the defeat, as if he had been naive enough to imagine that things could still proceed as they had during normal times.

At that moment Monsieur Saussier came up to him.

"Don't lose patience, Monsieur Bridet. And that reminds me of something I'd forgot to talk to you about, the Hotel des Deux-Sources—you didn't tell me that you weren't staying there anymore."

"I checked out this morning."

"Why was that?"

"I was planning to go back to Lyon this evening."

"And your luggage?"

"I left it at a café near the station."

"I see. You must excuse my prying, for this afternoon one of our inspectors made a trip there to your hotel only to hear that you had left, that you'd taken your belongings."

Sounds of voices from the foyer interrupted Monsieur Saussier. He turned around. Monsieur Schlessinger had risen to his feet. Two men, visible from the back, could be seen speaking to invisible interlocutors.

"Here they are!" cried out Monsieur Saussier. To Bridet he announced: "You're going to see your friend Basson."

It was then that Bridet suddenly understood what was happening. They had organized a confrontation. Everything was becoming clear. But to what end? What would he need to say?

Shortly after that Basson entered the room. Following him came Keruel de Mermor along with two men. Keruel motioned them to stand in the doorway. They obeyed with the indifferent docility of soldiers assigned to security. Bridet looked at Basson, endeavoring to catch his eye in the hope of reading some advice there. But Basson appeared not to see him. He was certainly not emerging from a dark place, yet his gaze had a strained and flitting quality, like someone walking into a courtroom where he is to be tried for a crime. There was nothing changed in his outward look, in his manner, his physical self had not been affected; but an expression of extraordinary gravity, as though he had had a face-to-face encounter with death or some horrible calamity, had been inscribed upon his features, not at that very instant but, you could tell, some number of hours ago.

He advanced, head up, in appearance very much in control of himself. The light, coming from the little middle-class street, had spread over him. Bridet was struck by a surprising detail: Basson seemed to be younger. His paleness seemed that of a young girl. His face was unlined. His features had become finer. Fear or inner turmoil had had the unexpected power of divesting those features of their ordinarily heavy and material qualities.

Bridet lifted his chin to attract his friend's attention. The latter did not see him, or rather (at least such was Bridet's impression) did not want to see him. Plainly Basson was putting on an aristocratic imperturbability before these associates of his, and as for this friend from the past whom they wanted to put on the stand against him, Basson disdained even to acknowledge him. He gazed at Saussier, and was told: "It's not with me you are going to have to deal, but with Monsieur Schlessinger."

"Very well," Basson replied, planting himself opposite the desk.

Was it because his heart was beating faster and harder? Anyhow, in the pouches under Basson's eyes one noticed the regular pulsing of an artery. Bridet didn't know what to do. He ought perhaps to have stood up, shaken his friend's hand, pretended not to understand any of this, but he didn't have the strength. For all that he was incapable of taking his eyes off him. All at once he noticed that Basson was unconsciously keeping his mouth part way open, not in one of those ordinary pouts meant to proclaim detachment, but in order to facilitate his breathing.

"Why doesn't he close his mouth?" Bridet wondered, wincing to see his friend, struggling with all his might to create the illusion of complete self-control, give himself away with a detail so easy to correct.

"Sit down," Schlessinger said to him harshly.

"There's no need," answered Basson.

An instant later the gap between his lips was there again. Ten men were in the room. Nevertheless a sudden silence fell upon it, revealing that throughout the preceding hubbub the business at hand had not ceased to be in the forefront of everyone's thoughts.

"Please step this way, Monsieur Bridet," Schlesinger said.

Bridet realized that he alone had remained sitting down. He sprang to his feet. Now he was standing next to Basson and facing the desk.

"Are you or are you not acquainted?" Schlessinger demanded, as though irritated by a charade that had gone on for too long.

Bridet and Basson looked at one another openly for the first time.

Bridet hesitated for a moment. He had just had the sudden feeling that he had not been acting naturally; connected with Basson as everyone knew that he was, he ought to have spoken to him right away without being invited, ought even to have held out his hand.

Basson too said nothing. He looked his old friend up and down, then, as if this question had been asked in regard to the very barest of acquaintances, he answered coldly: "I do indeed know Monsieur Bridet."

"Yes, yes, we're acquainted," said the latter.

Basson remained impassive. He wasn't denying that he knew Bridet, but he communicated his contempt for this police ruse of seeking to get at him through the intermediary of a friend. He did not hold it against that friend for taking part in the proceeding. But with his coldness he was showing the policemen that they were wasting their time, that his feeling for this friend from his past wasn't of such importance as to unsettle him in what he had to say in his defense.

Schlessinger opened his briefcase. He withdrew no papers from it.

"You state," he said to the two men, "that you never met in Lyon."

"I do," exclaimed Bridet, thrilled to be telling the truth.

Basson made no answer. By his scornful air he intimated that if this was all they had to ask him he saw no point in responding.

This attitude must have annoyed Schlessinger, for he then had at Basson alone: "Didn't you want to send your friend Bridet to Africa?"

"He asked me to, he was the one who wanted it."

"How come you gave him a safe-conduct pass? And after having been supplied with the most unfavorable reports about him?"

"I had no knowledge of those reports until afterwards. Once I did I showed him the door. When he came to see me yesterday I told him I had no answer."

"Yes, but you didn't notify the department. It was all handled as though you wanted this departure to take place without your knowing about it. Didn't you plan on using Bridet as a messenger?"

"Never."

"Oh, never!" Bridet confirmed.

"You say," continued Schlessinger, "that you showed him the door. But it's curious that before doing so you would wait until we had got our hands on your Lisbon telegrams."

Basson ran his tongue over his lips. He was perspiring, but only a very little . No beads of sweat upon his face, but a sort of moist film like the trace a damp cloth leaves on marble.

"Bridet asked me for a safe-conduct pass, which I refused him. Period," said Basson. "Supposing I was to have had some need of an agent, please believe that I'd have made a better choice of one. As for the telegrams from Lisbon, that's another matter."

Schlessinger turned toward Bridet: "And so what were you forever doing at the Ministry of the Interior? And that trip to Lyon? A safe-conduct pass doesn't require that amount of applying, that many comings and goings, especially when you're a friend of Monsieur Basson."

"I was always asked to come back. I now understand why. As he just said, Monsieur Basson never had any intention of issuing me a safe-conduct pass. He kept me hanging about, not daring, out of friendship, to give me a formal refusal."

Bridet had uttered these words in a tone of bitterness. In reality, since he had had the revelation that Basson

[93]

thought as he did, was acting against Vichy, he felt himself swept by an immense urge to serve him, to dedicate himself to him, to show Basson that he was faithful in his friendship. But he didn't dare do it. Intuition told him that this was precisely what Basson was dreading, that the latter's coldness, this wish to keep him at a distance, came from his fearing that he would be more compromised than helped.

"Monsieur Bridet may step out, I believe. We haven't yet received our visit from the female informer I spoke to you about," interrupted Monsieur Saussier. "She's due to arrive this evening on the seven o'clock train. Her testimony will be of very great value to us. If I learn anything I'll have Monsieur Bridet notified. For the moment I'd say that the best would be to try and clear up this telegram business."

"Don't forget that tomorrow evening I'm leaving for Paris, and I won't be back until Saturday," said Schlessinger. Then, turning to Bridet, he added: "You can be off, Monsieur Bridet. Come back tomorrow morning."

Bridet was so happy to be free, and what had befallen him was so unexpected after all that turmoil of emotions, that he could not conceal his joy, despite the shame he felt at displaying it and of appearing to acknowledge, without having made more of a protest, that up until this minute he had stood deprived of his liberty.

"Thank you, thank you," he said with that need for love or rather for fraternity, with that expression of gratitude, of candor, of deep sincerity to which policemen attach no importance when their chief considers you guilty, but which stirs them when coming from a man to whom justice has been rendered.

"You have no reason to thank us," said Schlessinger, addressing Bridet as if he were some crank.

"Do come and see me," said Basson without hiding a touch of contempt for his old friend who was so little able to exercise command over himself, and especially in order to show all these policemen how sure he was of the favorable outcome of this investigation .

Bridet headed toward the door. All the self-assurance he had lost during the course of this appalling day had returned to him. He stopped to light a cigarette. Now that he was free, he didn't want to look as if he were in a hurry to leave; he even experienced an incomprehensible urge to linger, to witness what was to follow. When about to leave the room he couldn't help turning around and saying something further to Schlessinger.

He was but a few paces from the desk when he heard the top level police official, who hadn't anticipated this odd turn of affairs, say to Saussier, without raising his nose from his papers: "Just excess baggage, that Bridet of yours . . ."

This not very flattering opinion didn't halt Bridet. He wanted to come across as never having doubted that truth would triumph. The best way of displaying his confidence was to show that he stuck to his guns. He had come to Vichy to ask for a safe-conduct pass. Were they finally going to give him one? Again he went up to the desk. Basson didn't look at him. His mouth was still open. From time to time he brought his hand briskly up to his face as if a fly were bothering him. It was not a fly, but rather the isolated drops of sweat that were now trickling down his skin.

"Excuse me," said Bridet in the tone of a man seeking to increase the underlying sympathy he believes he has inspired, "I wanted to say two things to you. You asked me to come back tomorrow morning. Would you like me to come around ten o'clock? Also I wanted to talk to you about my papers. But I'll talk to you about that tomorrow. I see that you don't have the time."

"Yes, ten o'clock, perfect," said Schlessinger, raising his eyes and looking at Bridet as if he no longer quite knew who he was.

The latter left the room. While moving quickly across the vestibule, he heard: "One second, Monsieur Bridet."

He recognized the voice as that of the Bourgoing he had been obliged to eat lunch with and who was in the midst of chatting with a colleague. Bridet turned around, simulating deep surprise. "Do you have something to tell me?" he asked.

"Have you been given permission to leave?" Bourgoing asked.

"Yes."

"Well, that's news to me."

The inspector turned to his colleague .

"Do you know about it?"

Bridet, who had never been a figure of any great importance, now feared having subalterns make a victim of him as had happened on so many occasions in his life.

"I've just taken leave of Monsieur Schlessinger," he said sharply.

"Yes, that's possible, but Monsieur Schlessinger hasn't said anything to me."

"I repeat that I've just left him."

The two inspectors glanced at each other.

"Go find out," said one of them.

"There's no cause for such zeal," Bridet remarked.

"Oh, it's better if I go," said Bourgoing.

"My God, how you love to complicate matters," said Bridet to the inspector who had remained with him.

Shortly afterward Bourgoing came back.

"A good thing I went to find out," he said. "We've got to take him you know where. Monsieur Saussier said so."

"And Monsieur Schlessinger?" asked Bridet, once more invaded by worry.

"Don't talk to me about that one . . . He was within an inch of giving me the sack."

CHAPTER 10

They dined in the restaurant where they had had lunch. This establishment had clearly come into good favor with the police. Bridet wondered what they had in store for him. His companions were being very nice. Their attitude was one of great deference. For example, they let him pick out a table. They were served an aperitif, and then another on the sly, because it wasn't daytime. Even though his situation wasn't quite as good as it had been at noon, Bridet felt relieved. The day was over with, and nothing more could happen to him before tomorrow. He started up a conversation with his two guards. They didn't seem to view their prisoner as a dangerous character. "That makes their job easier," thought Bridet.

They did not seem to doubt that he would be released and their attentions in his regard suggested that they were trying to win his favor. Perhaps Bridet was protected in high places. They obeyed their superiors, but they were always mindful that through no telling what shift in developments the situation could be reversed.

In the evening the atmosphere is always more cordial. At the end of the dinner the owner came over to sit for a moment at their table. Bridet was now pretty optimistic. Nothing distinguished his group from others nearby.

These inspectors were good fellows, they really were. They were behaving more and more as if Bridet were going to be freed the next day, as if they had to take advantage of the circumstances to foster a friendship which might prove useful later on.

They came round to talking about what they were going to do with Bridet overnight, but in the tones of men who are obliged also to forsake their own beds and as if the same mischance had befallen all three of them.

Notwithstanding, dinner over with, they conducted Bridet to the neighboring police station, carrying on like people who are annoyed at not being able to go home to bed. The whole thing, they grumbled, was "just a bit too much to take."

It was half past eight. It had been dark for a long time. Five or six uniformed officers were chatting in the guard room. When the newcomers reported in they didn't budge. Bourgoing asked whether the lieutenant was there. On hearing a policeman reply in the negative he didn't appear put out. "We're here to spend the night," he said. The officers looked at Bridet, not as at an offender or an ordinary criminal, but as at a man fallen into temporary disgrace and of whom there was no way of knowing whether he might not recover his lost favor by tomorrow morning.

One of them, however, maintained an ugly expression. He had, one could tell, a deep hatred for anyone, whatever sort of man he was, who had anything to do with the ruling circles. In his eyes, Bridet was one such person. These were the men who had lost the war, these were the ones who at this very moment, instead of being led straight to the firing squad, were continuing to make themselves feared and were being treated like princes, for basically they still retained their power even when in the hands of the authorities.

The policemen made room for the new arrivals. The man who had glowered at Bridet started talking in whispers. His colleagues looked ill at ease, then, suddenly becoming less amiable, they gathered in a corner of the station.

Bourgoing asked whether they didn't have a deck of cards. They answered grudgingly. "I'll try and find one," said the other inspector. He came back a little later with a brand-new pack that he must have bought in a nearby tobacco store. This freedom given his guards to expend small sums on his comfort or his recreation struck Bridet as very disturbing. It was to be classified among those attentions coming from higher up which tend to add something further to the gravity of the charges that have been filed. One would have thought that given the position that was his on the scale of things it hardly mattered whether Bridet ate chicken or not. They designed no ill against his physical person. The problem was more serious.

Bridet did not know a single game of cards. The policemen taught him *belote*. It was tough going. Despite all his honest effort he couldn't manage to keep a single rule in his head what with all that was on his mind already. And for over an hour he had the disagreeable sensation, generated by his inability to learn, that he was displaying in plain view of everybody the anxiousness that was gnawing him within. In the end he said jokingly: "I'm stopping. The two of you play together. I'll referee."

At that moment the captain's secretary entered the room. He walked up to the three men but didn't look at Bridet. "Who's winning?" he asked. Then he withdrew without appearing to have registered the prisoner's presence. It seemed that there was nothing special about his being there. Unknown persons must often be brought in this way to spend the night. By this indifference of his for the person under watch the secretary was plainly trying to show that he wasn't second-guessing the future and that he was wary of these chance comraderies whose consequences could not be foreseen.

At ten o'clock two cyclist policemen back from their rounds entered the station. They didn't speak to the inspectors. Bridet overheard them asking which of the three was the accused. Somebody must have explained because shortly afterward Bridet noticed those cyclists eyeing him with curiosity.

A half-hour later the two inspectors stopped playing.

"And the blankets?" one of them asked.

"The fact is we don't have any," said an officer with the ungraciousness typifying employees for whom the most insignificant task not included within their "assigned duties" assumes unthinkable proportions.

"But we've got to have some," said the inspector. "This gentleman isn't going to just spend the night the way he is," said Bourgoing.

The inspectors' rising to his defense once again caused Bridet deep misgivings. It was so very artificial. No matter if it looked sincere, once you knew the situation Bridet was really in vis-à-vis his guards, it was hard to take seriously. And he listened with the most complete indifference to the bitter-sweet words that rang out.

Suddenly the secretary reappeared.

"Come with me for a minute," he said to Bourgoing.

Bridet was more and more nervous. He was getting the feeling this was all some sort of performance on the part of the inspectors whose aim was to get him locked up in a cell so that, once rid of him, they could go off and spend a peaceful night in their own beds until morning. They obviously had no such orders but they were going to make it appear as if there hadn't been anything else they could do .

A short time later Bourgoing came back.

"You can keep 'em, your blankets!" he told the officers.

Then turning toward his colleague and Bridet he added: "The boss wants us."

"Now?"cried out the inspector in surprise.

"Yes, that's how it is."

Bridet looked at the two men in an attempt to glean from their faces whether this was good or bad news.

"How do you . . . explain it?" he asked, in two separate breaths.

"No idea at all."

"It's curious," Bridet observed.

All at once he felt that the so-called friendship that had established itself between the two inspectors and himself had just faded away; that now, unlike the way it had been a short while ago, his guards were doing no more than carrying out orders; that they had turned back into what they were paid to be.

On walking out into the night he was stricken with fear. To be steered from one office to another, to wait, to undergo questioning was trying enough in broad daylight, but at night when it seemed that all activity ought to be suspended, it had something infinitely more threatening about it. In daytime all the minor clerks, all those people coming and going in the very heart of police headquarters were a sort of guarantee. But at present, with the offices deserted and everybody in bed, he was as good as at the mercy of one or two persons.

"Does it often happen," Bridet asked in an off-hand way, "that Monsieur Saussier questions people at night?"

"It's the first time," an inspector said.

Bridet felt a weariness in his thighs.

"What's happened, do you suppose?"

"No idea at all," said the inspector. "It's just our job to obey."

"You won't leave me . . ."

These words had escaped from Bridet. In his distress, before the mystery of what was awaiting him in the deserted premises of the police, he had not been able to prevent himself from clinging to these two men who, uncaring as they might be, had despite everything a certain consciousness of good and evil.

On Rue Lucas the windows were dark.

"There's some mistake," one inspector said. "It's not possible. Everybody's gone. Go find out . . ."

The other inspector made his way into the building. He came back a short time later.

"Yes, it's all right, they're waiting for us. They're in Keruel's office."

The two plainclothesmen had Bridet walk in front, then shut the door behind them. There was no light switch. By the flame of a cigarette lighter they started up the stairway. Bridet had to lean on the banister for a moment.

"Come on, come on, keep climbing, do what you're told," Bourgoing shouted, abruptly transformed.

Bourgoing was at the rear. Bridet had just overheard him say to his colleague that Saussier wasn't happy about having him, Bourgoing, come in and ask whether the order to bring the prisoner had really been given.

"Bastard," muttered Bridet.

"What did you say?" asked Bourgoing.

"Nothing," answered Bridet. "Only that I'm winded."

"Watch out. Don't try pulling anything, I'm warning you I won't let you get away with it."

At the second floor Bridet stopped.

"One floor to go," said Bourgoing, "and no funny business."

"So they have the whole house," exclaimed Bridet. "The mezzanine, the second floor, the third . . ."

"Don't worry yourself about that."

The suite was dark. However, one saw a glimmer of light at the end of the hall. Saussier and Keruel were sitting in a modest little room lit only by the lamp on the desk. They resembled a pair of directors of some commercial firm peacefully checking the books while their employees were gone.

"Come in, Monsieur Bridet," said Saussier with unexpected friendliness.

One would have said that a new fact in Bridet's favor had come to light and that, having himself never doubted that it would, Saussier was glad to talk to him about it as he had always wanted to be able to do.

"Monsieur de Keruel, Monsieur Outhenin and I have just had a long conversation with your wife," continued Saussier.

"With my wife!" cried Bridet.

"Yes, but allow me to finish. What she told us exactly squares with what you told us yourself. I thought you would be happy to see her again this very evening," Saussier went on with that faintly condescending respect officers show toward the conjugal duties of their men. "That's why, despite the lateness of the hour, I had you come, certain that with such a reason in mind you wouldn't hold it against me. Your wife's staying at the hotel, now hold on . . ."

"The Hotel des Etrangers," said Keruel.

"She's waiting for you. The only thing I'll ask of you, Monsieur Bridet, is to kindly come back tomorrow morning, not here, but one floor below. Monsieur Schlessinger, whom I wasn't able to notify, still has certain minor matters to settle with you. Besides I'll be at the meeting."

"But how come my wife's in Vichy?"

"You'll ask her yourself in a little while. She'll be able to give you a better answer than I," Saussier replied, his smile full of innuendo.

It was so very obvious that Bridet let the matter drop.

"Until tomorrow then, Monsieur Bridet. Remind your wife she promised us she'd come as well."

Bridet shook hands all around.

"I'm happy for you and for myself," said Bourgoing, showing him to the door of the suite. "These are chores we really don't like being saddled with. We do want to protect order, but without serving as instruments for political vendettas. You do understand, don't you, Monsieur Bridet? Each man has got to do his job."

CHAPTER 11

Bridet asked a passer-by where to find the Hotel des Etrangers. It was a moonless night. The stars were out in such great numbers that Bridet's first impression was that the sky was hidden by mist. It took him a moment to realize that, on the contrary, the air was limpid and that the mist he saw was the stars themselves. Every now and again he turned around, unable to believe he wasn't being followed. Street lamps shone among the trees. His joy at being free was not complete however. He wondered both how it happened that his wife had come to Vichy, and how this simple fact might have sufficed to get him re- leased. It was odd. He thought of Saussier. Saussier had asked him to come back the next day. Things seemed to be looking a bit as if, someone having vouched for him, there were no further need to hold him in custody; as if Yolande had provided every necessary guarantee, as if she had served as surety so to speak, and also as if, by loos- ening their grip, by permitting him to taste again the sweetness of life, the police were counting on getting what they wanted out of him more easily. For was it not very strange indeed that at ten-thirty p.m., after deciding to have him spend the night at the station, they should change their minds. It was most certainly not some be-

lated remorse or the sudden emergence of some fact proving his innocence that accounted for such generosity.
They wouldn't have gone to this trouble for so little. They
certainly would have felt they could afford to wait until
the next day. It was all very peculiar. Yolande had obviously pleaded his cause. But what had she been able to
invoke and muster, and what was the source of the power
she had just displayed?

As he was walking along the dread mounted in Bridet
that his wife had committed a new blunder, that she had
defended him clumsily, that she had offered herself as
guarantee for his loyalty, and that she would aggravate his
problems tomorrow by getting herself arrested too as his
accomplice. She had been capable, with this thoughtless-
ness of hers, with her crazy belief that no one ever verified
what she said, of offering non-existent evidence of her
husband's fidelity to the Marshal. And tomorrow morning it would all collapse. He would look as if he had
wanted to deceive the police, as if he had instructed his
wife to do this.

Such was Bridet's line of thinking when he arrived at
the hotel. No, it couldn't be. He knew Yolande. She had
always been pro-Hitler, that was true. Before the war she
had often said: "What we need in this country is a Hitler." But she wasn't stupid. She knew full well that Pétain
wasn't any Hitler. To begin with he was too old.

Yolande was in bed. She had hung up her clothes and
put her things neatly away. She was propped up against
the pillow. The bedside lamp was on.

"Oh, I'm so happy to see you!" she cried as soon as
Bridet set foot in the room.

She didn't get out of bed but sat up to give her husband
a kiss. Then she sank back as if, now that Bridet was
here, she could completely relax. She had been so awfully

afraid . . . They had promised to release her husband that very evening, but on not seeing him return she feared they'd not kept their word. She had just lived through two awful hours, but there shouldn't be any more thinking about that since it was over, since he was here . . . Ah, how happy she was!

"It's beyond me, what's been going on. I don't understand anything," Bridet said.

"There's nothing to understand," Yolande said.

"How did you get here? What happened?" asked Bridet.

"I've already told you. Outhenin telephoned me."

"Why?"

"I'll explain it to you, darling. For now just let me be happy. Put yourself in my place. Aren't you pleased? Everything's settled, darling."

Bridet sat down in the armchair. His wife's joy did not reassure him in the least. The contacts he had just had with the police were far too serious for his suspicion to vanish upon a mere assertion from Yolande. He needed to know. For the moment he considered that nothing had changed. The police's mansuetude was hiding something. They must have tricked Yolande. They were using her. And this honest girl didn't want to tell him exactly what had transpired! Yes, without any doubt, at present he was utterly convinced of it, she was being used. This was just the sort of method those gentlemen employed. When you can't unmask people you get at them indirectly by way of persons who are dear to them. It's the classic ploy. They must have treated Yolande with all sorts of consideration. You are always sure to win a woman over by such means. Underneath all this was quicksand. They were throwing him into Yolande's arms. If that didn't give results, well then, tomorrow, at daybreak, they'd arrest the two of them.

"Listen to me, Yolande," said Bridet calmly. "You're going to tell me exactly what happened, in every single detail."

"Right away? Already? You don't want to sit down on the bed beside me?"

"Yes, right away."

"I'll tell you. You'll see, it's very simple."

"No, no, don't tell me anything. Answer my questions. When did Outhenin phone you?"

"Today, this morning, at eleven. I wasn't in. He called again at noon. As chance would have it I was there that time."

"What were his exact words?"

"He told me that he absolutely wanted to see me about you, that I should come immediately. Right away I thought that you had done something silly. I took the train."

"And you saw Outhenin?"

"Yes. He gave me a very nice welcome. A certain Monsieur Saussier and another gentleman who wasn't introduced to me were there as well. I was nervous. I had good cause to be. They noticed it. They comforted me, they explained that as far as they were concerned they knew you hadn't done anything, but that you'd placed yourself in a bad position. They asked me to tell them frankly what I knew about your relationship with Basson. I told them."

"What did you tell them?"

"The truth . . ."

"What truth?"

"I told them that all you'd wanted was to obtain a safe-conduct pass from Basson. They asked me if I knew what you wanted to do in Africa. I told them you wanted to serve the Marshal. They began to laugh so spontaneously that I realized they were smarter than you. Nobody was taken in by your act. Everybody had been able to tell that you were looking to join de Gaulle. 'Let your husband be a communist,' Outhenin told me, 'a Jew, a Gaullist, a Free Mason, or all of them rolled up in one, there's nothing we can do about it. But tell him not to take us for fools . . .' "

"What did you answer?"

"What would you have had me answer? I couldn't answer anything. I simply repeated that as far as Basson went, you didn't know he was in contact with de Gaulle. They asked me if you told me about the things you were doing. I answered: 'Yes.' That was when I added: 'Believe me, Basson is too intelligent to open up to a man like my husband. You yourself say that everybody knew what my husband had come to Vichy to do. And you suppose Basson would have chosen such a man as his accomplice!' They wanted to know whether I had noticed anything odd about your behavior. I answered: 'Absolutely nothing. My husband had only one desire: his safe-conduct pass.' "

"In short, you told them that I wanted to join de Gaulle."

"I didn't tell them that. They knew it anyway. There's nothing I can do to help that. You've got only yourself to blame. They're so sure of it that Outhenin made this remark to me: he said 'We intended to have your husband expelled from Vichy, but he was too queer . . .' "

"They didn't know anything at all," Bridet shouted, "and now because of you, they know."

"I didn't tell them anything."

"You didn't even appear surprised."

"I would have looked like a lunatic."

"Now I'm in a fine mess," Bridet shouted even louder.

"Not at all. Everything's been taken care of. The proof

is that they let you go. There was nothing else for me to do but talk to them frankly. Above all I had to avoid trying to fool them. If I'd tried being foxy, they weren't going to let either one of us go. People know what's in each other's hearts, darling. Words don't hide anything. Just as you know what's in Saussier's mind, Saussier knows what's in yours. They liked my way of talking. They understood that basically you weren't dangerous."

Bridet started to pace back and forth, very rapidly. He was beside himself.

"So then, officially," he shouted, "I'm a Gaullist, huh? That takes care of that, huh? Well, it won't be long! You can say you've done a nice job. But you ought to have shown indignation, Yolande . . ."

"Everybody knew the truth, I repeat."

"They didn't know a thing . . . You may rest assured that if they'd known something, they wouldn't have gone through all that song and dance."

"Really now, I wasn't as clumsy as all that since it's thanks to me you're here ."

"Just until tomorrow morning. They're going to come tomorrow morning, I'm sure of it! Oh, you don't know them."

"You're wrong, darling. You've always taken people for idiots. Well, those people aren't any stupider than you are. They understood what you were about and they don't even hold it against you. Actually, were they Gaullists themselves I'd feel a lot more worried on your account."

Bridet nearly lost his temper. But it came to him then that further discussion was pointless. What was done was done. Yolande thought that he was getting into a better mood.

"Tomorrow," she said, "we'll go together and pay a call on Monsieur Saussier."

"Pay a call . . . Ah, so you call that 'paying a call.' We won't need to go to the trouble. It's more likely he who will be paying us a call."

"You're just talking through your hat. When you get over being angry you'll understand. This Monsieur Saussier's a very nice person, you'll see."

"Oh, I've met him!"

Bridet started to laugh. An unforseen aspect of his situation had just appeared to him. His wife's arrival simply made him look like a fool. As things were going, it was as though any opinion he might manifest, no matter how subversive, was inoffensive, as though he were some poor sap, a Gaullist indeed, but out of stupidity. All it took was to shake him up a bit, to throw a scare into him, and he'd be back on the right path.

"You've basically made me out to be some moron," he said, still laughing.

Yolande got angry.

"How can you say such a thing to me?"

"Yes, some half-wit, some moron, who took it into his head that he was a Gaullist because he heard 'Sambre and Meuse' on the London broadcast."

"And even if that were so, what's the difference to you?"

Bridet made no answer. It was clear that Yolande didn't understand that a man could have a higher ideal than the one embraced by the miserable people around him.

"You tried to pass for a Pétainist, didn't you? What can it matter to you to pass for a moron? All that counts is to get out of the jam you've got yourself into."

"If that's all it was," he said, "it wouldn't amount to anything."

"What do you mean?"

"I mean that you and I will be able to consider our-selves lucky if tomorrow morning somebody doesn't show up to arrest us both. Believe me, don't trust those fellows. They're Boches, you hear me? They're more Boche than the Boches themselves."

"Don't say that, darling. You don't know what's in their minds."

"I don't know what's in their minds, but I do know what they do. Anyway, let's drop the subject, what's done is done."

Bridet moved over to the bed, took his wife's hands and for a long while he gazed into her eyes. She didn't like that. She wasn't without frankness but owing to a sort of physical weakness she kept her eyes lowered when looked at that way, and when she raised them again you sensed that she was ashamed about this weakness.

"Listen to me, Yolande."

"I'm listening to you, darling," she said, taking advan-tage of these few words to avert her eyes once again.

"Saussier asked me to come back. He asked you too. Well, we just won't go. I'm certain that if I go back to see him he'll just not let me go again. They wanted to be clever. They released me. I'm going to take advantage of it and I'm going to be more clever than they."

"You can't do that," said Yolande.

Bridet continued without appearing to have heard his wife.

"Tomorrow morning we'll take the train. We'll go to Lyon, and from there to Paris. They are different people up there, you know. Once there, I'll manage to get over to England. I've been an idiot indeed, but not in the way you think. I've been an idiot for imagining that this national revolution was just eye-wash."

"Don't get worked up, darling," said Yolande, who didn't like that her husband talk about himself with unconstraint.

"In Paris I'll find Frenchmen, other Frenchmen, intelligent Frenchmen. And the Boches being there, there'll at least be some solidarity between one Frenchman and the next."

Bridet suddenly realized that up until that point he had been speaking in a loud voice. He felt a jolt of fear. Somebody could be listening in.

"You're right," said Yolande. "We'll leave. But an additional day won't make any difference. For once let's be smart. Since they're well disposed, let's take advantage of it. You're certainly more sure to be left in peace if you do what they ask of you. They'll stop mistrusting us. And after that you'll have a much greater chance of succeeding in whatever you undertake."

"Lower your voice," said Bridet.

Yolande looked at her husband with amazement.

"You're mad. Don't tell me you imagine they have you under surveillance in a place like this."

"I'm telling you to lower your voice."

They were silent for a long moment, then Yolande said: "We'll both go together and see Saussier."

Bridet did not respond. His thoughts were on something else. At last he muttered: "I've understood now. At bottom I lacked courage. I didn't want to run any risks. I wanted everything to be on the up and up, to have papers in my pocket, an official appointment. That was where I was wrong. I understand this now. When you really intend to do something you mustn't be afraid of exposing yourself to danger. Above all you mustn't ask anybody for anything. You mustn't count on anybody but yourself. I've understood. Vichy will have taught me a lesson. So we're agreed, Yolande, aren't we? Tomorrow we go back to Lyon. From there we go to Paris. Once in Paris I'll come up with some way of getting to the coast and then slipping across to England. It'll be more dangerous, but it'll be cleaner."

Yolande got out of her bed. She put on her coat and shoes in order not to walk barefoot in this rented room.

"I can't stop you from doing that, darling. But I find it unreasonable on your part to give way to impatience all the time. You wait around for three weeks and then the last day, just as everything's about to be settled, you act on a momentary impulse. How is that going to be helpful to you? They'll be furious. They'd made up their minds to leave you alone. They're going to believe that you're afraid. They're going to say to themselves: if he's afraid it's because he's guilty. They'll hunt you out. I'm warning you, they'll hunt you out. Well, do whatever you want, darling."

A weary expression came over Yolande's face. Truly, her husband was incorrigible. He was a stubborn man. He didn't see the advantages he could extract from a seeming submissiveness. As always he was headstrong and inflexible.

"That's going to have nasty consequences, I'm warning you," she said.

CHAPTER 12

Bridet arrived in Lyon at twenty minutes past one. The trip had seemed interminable. At every stop he had feared that policemen, notified by phone, would mount aboard the train, and every time it started again he had felt enormous relief.

That morning his departure had gone off as normally as could be. Despite his predictions, nobody had come looking for him. Yolande made no final attempt to hold him back. She'd even given him some pieces of advice. Finally, he having besought her to accompany him, she had told him that she didn't wish to behave impolitely toward people who had been so nice. "They'll hold you in order to oblige me to come back," Bridet had declared. "You don't know what you're talking about," was Yolande's reply. And they had decided that once the "indispensable" call had been paid, she would take the five o'clock train and reach Lyon that evening in her turn. Consequently her husband had no need to worry since he'd see her again that very same day.

Bridet spent the afternoon seeing people in an attempt to find a way of crossing the Demarcation Line, his mind on Yolande the whole time. "What's going on between them?" he kept wondering. Sometimes he would have a surge of anger. But in the end tenderness always won out when he would tell himself that if his wife was taking risks this way, it was essentially out of love.

His anxiety grew with each passing hour. What would he do if, despite her promise, Yolande failed to arrive on the evening train? He would only be able to conclude that she had been arrested. He would have no choice but to return to Vichy. And once again anger flared up in him. He had foreseen it. He had warned Yolande. Why hadn't she listened?

For a long time Bridet had known that a milkman, whose butter and eggs store was located on a little street behind the Marché des Jacobins, drove every morning in his minivan to a point near the Demarcation Line, taking along four, five or six people who wanted to sneak over into the Occupied Zone. The man was a patriot. In certain circles he was considered admirable. His behavior showed that there still existed Frenchmen who didn't lack courage.

Bridet would have preferred being introduced to the milkman, but he was in such a rush to leave Lyon that he gave up looking for an intermediary. Around five o'clock he made up his mind to betake himself to the milkman's shop alone. He'd surely be able to inspire confidence, to appear likeable. If there was anybody who didn't look as though he belonged to the police it was he.

The metal shutter in front was halfway down. Although the armistice was only four months old the entire retail trade in foodstuffs was subjected to so many regulations which so clearly profited the German needs that by way of obstruction merchants would close their shops for whatever absurd reason. The authorities had yet to require that shops, even empty ones, remain open.

Bridet felt himself waver for a moment. What sort of

welcome was he going to be given? When he mentioned the Demarcation Line the milkman might pretend not to understand him. "Too bad, let's give it a try all the same," Bridet murmured. Stooping, he ducked under the metal shutter. In the dark store there was nobody. He called out. A woman appeared. Bridet was readying himself to enter into lengthy explanations that would enable her to guess what he was after when she said: "Wait a moment, my husband's on his way down." Indeed, shortly after, a big man arrived. "You want to leave tomorrow morning?" he asked immediately. "Yes," answered Bridet, astonished that his interlocutor would take so few precautions. "That's perfect. It just so happens I've room for one more." "But the fact is there are two of us." "Well now, there's a problem." "You'll squeeze together," said the shopkeeper's wife. The milkman hesitated, then finally accepted. "Be here at seven o'clock."

The two men shook hands. Bridet was overjoyed. It was all arranged, there was nothing further for him to attend to. Nevertheless, deep down, he was a little disappointed. Not for having paid eight hundred francs for Yolande and himself, nor for having to hand over a like sum to the *passeurs* the next day. Rather the cause of his disappointment was that this clandestine agreement pretty much resembled a business deal. It would have been so much more comforting, so much more bracing had this milkman really been the patriot he was reputed to be, had he accepted the money only insofar as he needed it, had his action been a spontaneous and disinterested manifestation of resistance, and had one not felt that he was deriving a personal profit from his compatriots' unfortunate situation.

At eight o'clock Bridet betook himself to the Perrache train station. Such was his fear that, the last traveler having come through the gate, he be left standing alone, that Yolande not have been on the train, that he reproached himself for having proposed such a precise rendezvous. Would it not have been better that she rejoin him at the hotel? There were already several hundred people crowded together at the south and north exits. Bridet now feared something else, that Yolande might not be alone, that inspectors might have accompanied her from Vichy, knowing she was going to join her husband there.

The first passengers soon appeared. Suddenly he let out a cry of joy. Yolande was among them, smiling, all by herself. Yes, no doubt about it, she was alone. Behind her the passengers had stopped, were hugging relatives, going off in other directions.

"You see," she said, with a triumphant expression, "they didn't do anything to me."

"Yes, yes, I see," said Bridet, fondly taking her by the arm, high up, just below the armpit.

"Did they say anything to you?" he asked a few minutes later.

"Nothing. I knew they wouldn't. They'd have been happy to see us together, that's all."

"Did Saussier say anything about that? He didn't find it odd that I not come?"

"No. He simply said it was regrettable."

"Ah, he said it was regrettable," Bridet said anxiously.

"Right away we got onto another subject."

"But what did they want with me? What did you talk about?"

"He asked me where you were, when I was to see you again. I told him we were supposed to meet this evening."

"You told him that?"

"Naturally. There's nothing clumsier than to tell the truth only halfway. Either you lie, or you tell the truth.

They won't leave us be unless we act forthrightly with them. So I had no reason to hide from them that we had decided to return to Paris and resume a normal life."

"You told them we were going to Paris?"

"Yes, I certainly did, in your interest. Outhenin said he thought I was right. He felt that was the best thing for us to do. However, it would have been preferable had you come with me."

"Why?"

"In order to say all those things yourself. It might have had a more serious effect. Even though they were exceedingly nice I could very clearly sense that underneath they were a bit ruffled."

"From what?"

"From nothing. I just sensed it. I'm sorry but it always makes a bad impression when a man sends his wife in his place."

"I didn't send you. It was the opposite: I didn't want you to go."

"You know very well that it wasn't possible. The strength is all on their side, it's they who are in power. We don't know how long this thing is going to last. It may last ten years."

"You didn't mention England, at least?"

"There wasn't any reason to."

"I bet you did mention it, didn't you?"

"You're crazy."

Bridet paused for a moment. No, Yolande certainly had not spoken about England. Nonetheless he had the impression that she was far more under those people's sway than she was letting on, that in her dealings with them there circulated a rather bizarre image of him. They were strong; he was "one of the weak." No harm would be done him. Even better, they'd prevent him from doing any to himself, for example by joining General de Gaulle.

Abruptly changing his tone Bridet said: "Anyhow, all that's over with, let's not talk about it anymore. I got some good work done this afternoon. At seven o'clock tomorrow morning we're taking the milkman's van up to the Demarcation Line. Once we're on the other side of it and in Boche country, well, it's a sad thing to say, but we'll be able to breathe."

Yolande appeared dumbfounded.

"What do you mean?"

"That we're going to cross the Demarcation Line at Verdun-sur-le-Doubs."

"You have to obtain your *Ausweiss* first."

Bridet began to shout: "*Ein Ausweiss*! Come on, look at me. Look at me will you. You think I am going to go and ask for an *Ausweiss*? No by God, I'm not. I'd prefer to stay here."

"But darling, the Kommandantur will give it to you right away."

"To hell with the Kommandantur. We'll bloody well cross that way. Without anybody being the wiser. I don't want to have anything more to do either with the Boches or with Vichy. You understand that? I've had enough."

"All right," said Yolande, resigning herself out of diplomacy.

But a little later she added that she was unwilling to run the risk of three weeks in prison, of being shipped back over the line, getting on the blacklist.

"Therefore you mean to go and see the Boches and beg them for an *Ausweiss*?" asked Bridet.

She replied that he always exaggerated, that, with such an attitude, he was going to wind up in trouble. As for her

Ausweiss, she already had it. The Kommandantur had raised no objections. He need merely do as she had done. She even recounted a story about an elevator in the Carlton. She had found herself going up with some high-ranking Boche who immediately removed his hat and who though going to the second floor while she was going to the third, had gone on up to the third with her. He had opened the two doors of the elevator for her, he had bowed, then he had gone from the third down to the second on foot. "You can say whatever you like, no French officer would ever act that way with a woman he didn't know."

"Thank God! The French are neither ridiculous nor obsequious. As for me, my dear Yolande, I'd rather risk getting myself arrested at the Demarcation Line than take the elevator at the Carlton. It's a question of character."

That evening, in their hotel room, they stopped talking about their divergences. Each was going to act according to his own lights. After seven years of marriage, an intelligent couple ends up mutually respecting one another's will without ceasing to love each other on that account. Bridet would leave in the van, since he insisted on it; for her part, Yolande, a few days hence, would take the night train, the Paris express as it was called, although it would be held up in Moulins for several hours because of the formalities. She told her husband to take care of things in connection with the apartment, to go and pick up the valuables she had left in safekeeping with friends. There was the question of the trunk which was stored at an aunt's. There was also an "effect of snow" a Franche-Comté painter had given them—Zing was his name—which by now ought to be worth a bundle. She also asked him to go over to the Rue Saint-Florentin the same day he arrived. "Returning is the best thing we're doing, because you know, darling, the Boches have an eye on the apartments of those who don't return."

Yolande had spoken to him so often about her trunks, her valuables, her linen, that Bridet had paid no attention to her instructions. But when from her purse she drew the bunch of eighteen keys she had been dragging about, despite the weight, ever since her departure from Paris, he flared up suddenly.

"Oh no!" he cried! "Not by a long shot!"

"What's wrong?"

"If you think I'm going to live in the apartment, you're mistaken. Moreover it'd be madness on my part."

Yolande's look was one of deep surprise.

"I don't understand," she said.

"I'd rather not have them able to find me."

"But you have absolutely nothing to fear, darling. Nobody is out to harm you."

"They say that, I know. I prefer to take my precautions. I'm not going home. No point discussing it."

"And where do you intend to go?"

"I'm going to go to your brother's."

"Now that's a great choice. One would think you were trying to worsen your case. You seem to have a mania for that. Anyhow, you know who Robert is, I even wonder whether he isn't already in prison. He's capable of having planted a bomb—"

"I tend to gravitate—naturally enough—toward congenial surroundings, where my way of thinking is shared."

Yolande lit a cigarette. All of a sudden she spoke up again: "I'm going to tell you something, and don't be hurt by what I say. You are grotesque, absolutely grotesque. You're like all those people who imagine that because the Boches are here, they are going to be arrested. They have done nothing whatever and they sneak around on tip-toe.

They want to make themselves interesting. Nobody knows them, nobody pays attention to them and they both hide and keep up their flagrant wig-wagging. For an intelligent man like you to get into these habits—well, it's sad. And the funniest part is that finally such people really do get arrested."

CHAPTER 13

Bridet arrived at the Demarcation Line the next day at ten o'clock. He noted that it was more the *passeur* than he who belonged to the category of people Yolande had alluded to the night before. This *passeur* so cloaked himself in mystery that you would have thought that he was about to affront the greatest dangers there are. They waited for nightfall. He gathered everyone together in the back room of the café. All day long Bridet had heard it said that the Boches were harsher by far on people slipping from the unoccupied to the Occupied Zone than on the others. The unoccupied zone was a cesspool. Everybody knew that. It was natural that they not let anybody out of it. So, as always, it was because of those Jews and those communists that decent people had to suffer.

Women, children, old people were seated around tables bare of any drinks. One lone lamp was lit. Bridet was resentful toward the milkman for having taken them here. He began to get uneasy, not because of the eventual danger, but because of the familial turn this expedition had taken on. He drew the *passeur* aside and asked whether there wasn't some way of crossing the line by himself. The *passeur* answered him in a voice loud enough for everybody to hear that if he wasn't up to it he

[125]

had better go back to Lyon. Family groups, posed like aristocrats at the Conciergerie, directed upon Bridet the gaze of people who see new complications arise in moments of peril.

An old man went up to him: "Monsieur, all of us here are in the same situation. I do hope you're not going to render this good man's task any more difficult." A child, sensing that things weren't going well, started crying. Bridet sat back down. He was seized by fear. All these fine people were going to get picked up after not even attempting to escape. And they would be very quickly released. The Germans saw perfectly well with whom they were dealing. But as for himself, he'd be in their clutches for good. Where to go? What to do? He was in unfamiliar country and there wasn't even a moon. Now that he'd got himself into this fix he had to stay there.

They were waiting for all sorts of favorable conditions, for the sentries' round to be over, for another *passeur* to arrive at the meeting place. In the end, unable to sit still any longer, Bridet wanted to step outside, to be alone. He headed for the door. A great commotion arose among the persons present. Bridet was going to make everything go awry. It was shameful. The *passeur* caught him by the arm and ordered him not to go out. He shouted that he was the man in charge. Bridet returned to his chair. Then he heard some women saying that it was truly deplorable that a young man should show fear to this extent, that it was no longer any wonder to them that their poor France was in such straits.

Extraordinary as it may seem, Bridet felt enormously relieved once he found himself in the Occupied Zone. Despite the similarities between the buffet of the little station where he was now waiting for the Paris train and the café where he had spent several hours on the other side of the Demarcation Line, he felt well up inside him the emotion the exile feels upon rejoining his compatriots at last. He was proud to exchange a few insignificant words with the clerk, the station employees, the travelers. He was speaking to Frenchmen whose fate he shared. Childishly he even hid from them the fact that he had come from the unoccupied zone, it appearing to him so shameful to have been dispensed from common hardships.

He reached Paris the following morning. The streets were empty. He decided to go to Robert's on foot. Owing to the absence of other means of transportation, there was an enormous press at certain metro entrances. Some streets were choked with pedestrians, whereas others, although very close by, were deserted. This obligation everyone was under to do the same thing provided a first taste of what the occupation was. But what struck Bridet even more was the sight, upon almost every wall, of countless scribblings, drawings, and of graffiti of all sorts proclaiming the Parisians' fractious character. "Death to the Boches"—from those inocuous inscriptions emanated a great sadness. You felt that it was the only bit of freedom they had not been able to take away from the citizens of Paris and that at least they were putting it to some purpose.

Bridet had told his wife that he wouldn't go to the shop. Nevertheless he made a detour that took him by Rue Saint-Florentin. He saw the little shop with its lowered metal shutter upon which, as upon so many others, a thick layer of rust-tinted grime had settled. The other stores were closed as well. Were they also to re-open soon, like Yolande's?

At length Bridet arrived at Robert's. He asked him right away whether there wasn't someone among his friends who might own a property on the Channel coast. He advised Robert of his plan. He wanted to get over to England as quickly as possible. After that he told him about Vichy, the difficulties he had experienced. "It doesn't surprise me," Robert remarked. Since he hadn't answered his initial question Bridet returned to the attack. Robert looked uncomfortable. Finally he said that he didn't remember having any friends living by the seashore.

Bridet was properly amazed at his brother-in-law's attitude. His memory of Robert had been of one of those righteous, independent, faintly envious men of whom it is said that their honesty stands in the way of their succeeding. It had seemed to Bridet that the Robert who, before the war, used to detect behind the behavior of the majority of his fellow men an intolerable need for authority, who in regard to Hitler had harbored an almost personal hatred, would have got himself condemned to solitary confinement rather than rub shoulders with a German. Nothing of the kind. Barely one hour after arriving Bridet had grasped that his brother-in-law, very far from rising up with all his might against the occupant, had seen in this presence a means of avenging himself upon his compatriots and of achieving the position which, he believed, had long been due him.

Bridet spent the whole of the following day seeing old friends again. He was disappointed by the reception he received. He ascertained that the bonds of friendship must be strong indeed in order to withstand the effects of a nation-wide calamity. He had thought that such a calamity would have induced a similar way of feeling and thinking in everybody. However, with each visit he paid, he had had the surprise of finding himself before a man who seemed the victim of a personal misfortune, and when he had sought to lessen his interlocutor's distress by saying that he was suffering as much as he, the man had listened distractedly, from this community of unhappiness deriving not the least bit of relief.

However, in the afternoon, he got together again with one of his former colleagues from the *Journal* who seemed to rejoice at the idea of giving it a shot and even volunteered to set out with him. He would award this business top priority, see to it they held all the aces in their hands, etc . . . Ah! how thrilled he would be when he didn't have to look at Germans anymore.

Despite his disappointments during the course of the day Bridet went to bed full of hope. But when he met up again with his old friend the next day, he found him much cooled down. Their plan was unfeasible. The coasts were patroled by Boche motorboats. They were bound to get caught. This so swift renunciation made a strong impact upon Bridet. So nobody really wanted to do anything! He returned home with a violent headache. Indeed, if you took a thorough look at the matter the Occupied Zone was little different from the other. On both sides, people were frightened and out only for themselves. It was finally Yolande who was right. People were as though anesthetized. The defeat had been so brutal that they had not yet regained their senses. You'd have said that they were grateful—no telling to whom—just to be still alive. The only advantage, it had to be said, was that he felt safer than in Vichy. He wasn't under surveillance. It was obvious that the French police had no real power, that it was getting its instructions solely from the Germans, and since the Germans' foremost preoccupation was to maintain the broad outlines of order, a Frenchmen who was neither a Jew nor a communist, who kept inconspicuous, could believe himself safe.

On the fourth day Bridet began to worry about Yolande's failure to arrive. What had happened? She had told him that she would reach Paris before he did. He thought about going to their Rue Demours apartment. She had perhaps gone there. She was cold-shouldering him because he had preferred staying at Robert's. But the thought of returning to the so familiar neighborhood of Les Ternes upset him so much that he chose to wait a little longer. Obviously, as he was coming to realize now, his sensitivity was laughable. He didn't seem to understand that the Germans, as Yolande had said, were there for ten years, and that before such a state of affairs his attitude was as ridiculous as, from the viewpoint of her cook, was that of the mistress of the house who doesn't want the chicken butchered in her presence.

The next day he found a message from his wife at last. She had come to Robert's place but he'd been out. She announced that she would be dropping by again towards five o'clock. Looking at her once more, seeing her busy and aglow, happy to have resumed her principal habits from before the war, despite his anger that she should be so oblivious to France's misfortunes he was nontheless profoundly gladdened. She was very excited. She hadn't come earlier because she wanted to attend to her business first. She had had her apartment cleaned, her store opened. Nothing had been taken. She had been over to the bank three times. In the afternoon she went to pick up Zing's "effect of snow." Of all that she talked with extraordinary volubility, as if nothing else existed and, as far as she was concerned, the war were over. "We had a close call, darling." The only thing left was the trunk, which was in a safe place. Yolande hesitated about having it moved. She was afraid the truck drivers might be questioned in the street. She thought that it would be better to transport the contents piecemeal, in several trips.

Then, when she had exhausted this topic and had quieted down, she asked her husband whether he had had a good trip. She pointed out abruptly that nothing any longer argued against his returning to his own address. Next she spoke about her departure from Lyon. Everybody had been marvelous. Some friends had seen her to the station. She had even had a berth. At the Demarcation Line they had barely glanced at her *Ausweiss*. And the train had been kept standing for only three hours.

Since Bridet had not responded to her invitation to return home she reiterated it. Bridet remarked that this would perhaps be dangerous. "You're a child!" she exclaimed. He had nothing to be afraid of in a big city like Paris. The police had other things to do than busy themselves over him. She had been told so yet again.

"By whom?" asked Bridet.

"Some friends."

"Some friends whom I trust?"

"After you left I ran into Outhenin, absolutely by chance. He declared to me that your case was definitely closed. Ah! by the way, I forgot to give you a sensational piece of news. Basson escaped. How? I don't know how he did it, but he escaped. It was Outhenin who told me. He had quite some expression on his face."

"Why, that's just wonderful!" exclaimed Bridet. "Basson is a tremendous fellow, no doubt about it. If you'd seen him when he was being questioned, such coolness, such aloofness . . . He was driving all those Vichyites out of their minds! They tried to act high and mighty with him but he put them right back in their places every time. He's really quite a character, you know . . ."

Yolande smiled skeptically.

"Don't exaggerate, darling. If he was able to escape, it's because they wanted him to."

"You're out of your mind."

"If they'd intended to keep hold of him, your dear friend Basson wouldn't have fared any better than the others. They allowed him to skip."

Despite all his affection for his wife, Bridet couldn't keep from looking at her with a sort of scornful pity. He was immediately sorry. To change the subject he took advantage of Yolande's request that he come back and said: "You know very well that it would be unwise, my love. All the more so now that Basson has got away. They're going to think that I know where he is."

"How tiresome you are! I repeat to you once again that you're no longer involved in anything whatsoever, your case is settled, closed, buried. I find it absolutely ridiculous to live separately on account of some non-existent danger. But it might be after all that you have some reason that you're not telling me," she concluded with a sly smile.

"Not at all, darling. Surely not! You're on the wrong track . . ."

Their discussion lasted another ten minutes or so. Finally Bridet yielded to his wife's arguments. Since he was going to leave the country—for he was sure that sooner or later he would find some way of getting over to England—he mustn't cause her any distress. She loved him. Once in

England, when would he see her again? But he warned her that he could be led to leave her on a moment's notice, without having the time even to say good-bye. "Here, in Paris, it's not like in Lyon," he added, without great conviction. He kept only meeting people who were intelligent and courageous. He felt that he had support. Certainly it wouldn't be long. Moreover she was right; he ought never to have gone to Vichy. He ought to have come directly to Paris as she had wished. He would already be in England.

She kissed him.

"You can trust me," she told him. "You know I've always given you good advice."

They went back to Rue Demours. Bridet was so affected by this neighborhood where he had spent so many years, a neighborhood that had formerly been so animated, that to keep from seeing it such as it was now he gave Yolande his arm on coming up from the metro and shut his eyes. She said to him: "What a milk-toast you are! One must look squarely at life." "I prefer not to," he said. "You don't change, darling."

Once inside the building Bridet thought that he would feel relief, that it would be over, that with an effort of imagination he would be able to believe that nothing had happened, that there were no Germans in Paris. But when he spied the concierge, he understood that he was deluding himself again. She said hello without any hint of joy upon seeing him again, as if she too were exempted from any show of amiability by a misfortune that had descended upon her alone.

Yolande spent the evening unfolding and refolding sheets. Bridet watched her without managing to muster the slightest interest in what she was doing. Since he felt so little upon being home, why had he come back? He put the question to Yolande. "Don't start that again," she answered. "Don't you believe it would have been better for no one to know where I am?" "Listen to me, darling. If you'd run any danger at all, do you imagine I would have been so stupid as to come and get you?"

CHAPTER 14

At about seven o'clock the next morning the bell sounded at the front door. Bridet thought that it was the bell in the adjoining apartment. Indeed it often happened, while they were in a conversation, or when a car drove down the street at the same moment, that they mistook one bell for the other.

"Is that us, do you think?" asked Bridet, who had gone into the bathroom to wash up.

Yolande, still in bed, answered: "I didn't hear anything."

At that instant the bell rang again, but much longer.

"Go and open the door," said Bridet, frightened.

Yolande got up.

"It's Robert who's already here for the trunk," she said, slipping on her dressing gown. "He tends to start the day early."

A little later Bridet opened the bathroom door a crack and peered through. He saw two men speaking to Yolande in the adjoining room. They were showing her a piece of paper.

"He's not here," said Yolande.

"The concierge just told us that he came back last night," said one of the men.

For an instant Bridet considered flight, but all he had on were his pajamas and slippers. Later he wondered why he hadn't run off even so. But it's extraordinary how little it takes to paralyze us when we're caught without warning. To comprehend that our life is in danger requires a lot of time, and later, when we're done for, with bitter regret we think back to the chance we missed. It would have been so easy to flee, yet we didn't. Because we were just in our slippers we let ourselves get captured. And now when we would cross France in our bare feet, it is too late.

Yolande's voice was so firm that he still had the hope the two strangers would go away. He pushed the door shut very quietly and waited. Indistinct words reached him. For one instant he thought about throwing on some clothes, then it dawned on him that if he was still dealing with the police none of that would prove of any use. Suddenly he heard Yolande calling him. So she had said he was here. So she hadn't been able to do otherwise. He picked up a towel to keep in countenance, and opened the door.

"This is what they brought for you," said Yolande, tendering him a piece of paper.

Printed in a modern cursive script, the letterhead on the large sheet had the look of having been written by a steady hand. He read:

Ministry of the Interior

———————————

Cabinet of the Minister

Lower down, in type whose clarity was that of an original copy: "By decision of the Minister of the Interior,

Monsieur Joseph Bridet, journalist, residing on Rue Demours, will be conducted to the Prison de la Santé, Boulévard Arago, and held in custody there."

Beneath that was the signature, with no authenticating
seal, for it was the minister himself who had signed.

"What!" Bridet exclaimed, trying to simulate instanta-
neous indignation.

What had just happened was so utterly inconceivable,
Yolande had been so glaringly mistaken, it was so pa-
tently obvious she had been wrong, that Bridet, despite
his anger, said nothing to her in the way of reproach. He
contented himself with staring at her fixedly and at
length. She wanted to cry, but her feminine self-esteem
restrained her. Her nerves were shaken, however, for upon
the surface of her skin one could make out a puckering
that sometimes lasted for several seconds and that resembled the wrinkles of old age.

She suddenly blew up. She did not acknowledge her
mistakes. She did not bewail herself for having more or
less handed her husband over. She was not overcome by
remorse. The evidence of her blunder led her to lash out,
not at herself, but instead at the two policemen. She
started to call them names. Were they not ashamed to be
doing such a job, Frenchmen that they were! Well, they
hadn't seen the last of her. She had connections. She
would find out very fast, by mid-day, whether they weren't
overstepping their rights. She'd pay a visit to their boss.
Sanctions would be taken. It made no difference that the
minister's signature was on the piece of paper they'd
shown her, she was convinced that piece of paper was a
fake. We hadn't yet reverted to the days of the *lettre de
cachet*. This smacked of some maneuver designed to cast
discredit upon the government. But she'd have the last
word in this matter. She'd go to see that minister. If that

didn't suffice she'd turn to the Germans. Yes, she'd turn to General Stulpnagel. She'd tell him the whole story. And she had no doubt at all about the conscientiousness with which this case would be looked into.

At the start, the inspectors were not daunted. They had tried, in good-natured tones, to calm Yolande. She was wrong to get angry. This was simply a mere formality. Every time they had been given a similar assignment things had subsequently worked out very nicely. The soundest course was to facilitate their task.

But when Yolande threatened to bring the German general into the picture, something incredible occurred. Abruptly, as if they had just heard words which true Frenchmen like themselves could not stand for from a fellow countryman, the two inspectors turned crimson. Madame Bridet should pay attention to what she said. She would have to "measure" her words, otherwise they were going to be obliged to make a report. There were certain things no Frenchwoman had any right to utter. It was an insult to all those who, in the calamity, were striving to save what could still be saved.

Bridet had got dressed. He had one thought only: of fleeing, and in order to conceal this, he had put on a docile and resigned air. At the height of the discussion he pretended to be looking for something. He opened a door. But the moment he stepped into the adjoining room, one inspector—the one with chiseled, rather handsome features but who looked nasty—instantly forgetting that he was in the midst of giving a lesson on patriotism to the mistress of the house, snapped: "Where are you going?" Bridet answered that he was looking for his money. "You don't need any money." Bridet yielded as if he did not in fact need any. "Let's go, come on," said the other inspector, the ruddy-faced, less mean-looking of the two.

On leaving the apartment Bridet once again looked at his wife as he had done a short while before. This is where her admiration for those Vichyite dandies had led her. They might never have given him another thought. It was Yolande, with all her chatter, who had little by little set them into motion. But she didn't seem to grasp the meaning of that look. She threw her arms around his neck, crying in a piercing voice: "Don't say anything, darling, let them do what they want. By tonight you'll be free and they'll be asking your forgiveness."

As they went down the stairway grew darker. Bridet was walking in front. The thought of springing forward, of dashing down the steps four at a time, flashed through his mind. Sizing up the policemen, he had felt that he could outrun them. But they must be armed. They would shoot. And wasn't there a third one below?

These considerations kept Bridet from acting and when, on the ground floor, he discovered that there was nobody, he was furious at himself. The concierge, suspecting something was up, pretended to be sweeping in front of the door. Bridet, who had never spoken to her, shook her hand.

"Are you going away?" asked the concierge in a sad voice wherein was apparent an interest that came from the heart.

Bridet made no answer. He had just descried a car parked a little farther on. It was a little old car with two seats and a broken windshield. The various administrations no longer had that first-rate pre-war equipment at their disposal. It was reserved for the Germans. And the modest everyday chores were carried out with makeshift means.

At the moment of climbing in Bridet was once again on the verge of making a break for it. If, while the inspectors were walking around the car, they had chanced to be on one side of it and he on the other, he wouldn't have hesitated. But this eventuality did not occur and, though he dragged his feet as long as possible, he finally had to seat himself between them.

Inside the Simca, with one inspector's arm behind his neck, not to prevent his escape, but for comfort's sake, Bridet pondered what had just happened. Yolande was the one who had absolutely insisted that he return to their marital domicile. A horrible suspicion suddenly entered his mind. The coincidence was extraordinary. The very next day after she came to get him two policemen had shown up at her door. You'd have thought that Yolande had had a hand in it. No, it wasn't possible. If there was any one person responsible it was he. One must never blame others when a calamity arises, only ourselves. "All I had to do was what I'd made up my mind to do," murmured Bridet. But what inkling could he have had of what was to happen? The French police had seemed to be absent from Paris. How could one have supposed that they still existed, with the Germans overseeing and controlling everything?

On arriving at the lock-up an odd incident occurred. As long as he had been at home, then out in the street, then in the car, as long as there had been in spite of everything some possibility of escaping, Bridet had remained very calm, precisely in order not to give himself away. But as soon as the prison door had been shut behind him, that calm yielded to anger. In the corridor, when he was being hustled forward a bit too familiarly, he suddenly halted, saying that he wouldn't walk one more step, that they had no right to arrest him, it was disgraceful, you just didn't arrest people without telling them what for. An inspector took him by the arm. Thereupon, losing all

[140]

control of his actions, Bridet wrenched himself free, shouting that he forbade anybody to touch him. Surprise was written on the faces of the surrounding policemen. At that point Bridet's conduct was so absurd that he appeared to everyone to have lost all sense of reality. Interpreting this instant of natural surprise as the sign that he was stronger than all these men combined, he had proceeded up to the door and, unaware how ludicrous his behavior was, had said to the officer standing guard there: "Open that door this instant!"

He didn't have time to get another word out. Two men grabbed him, saying: "Don't try any intimidation stuff with us!" Bridet started into a defensive crouch but received a slap. He was on the point of striking back, but all at once he realized that it was madness. Even though he felt the need to rub his cheek he didn't bring his hand up to his face.

"You're scum," he shouted.

The inspector with the fine features moved in on him, his hand raised: "Take back what you just said."

"You're scum," repeated Bridet.

The inspector broke into a laugh, pretending that in threatening him he had intended only to scare him.

CHAPTER 15

Contrary to custom, Bridet remained a very short while in the lock-up. He was first taken to the Criminal Records Office, but an administrative controversy broke out and they didn't proceed with the usual formalities. One could see that the functionaries were somewhat confused by the new jurisdiction. Bridet gazed at them coldly while they wrestled with their problems. Every moment or so he asked with a feigned seriousness: "What should I be doing? Do I wait for you?" They did not reply, sometimes forgetting they were dealing with a prisoner, absorbed as they were by their concern to cover themselves.

After being led down a very clean and electrically lit underground passage, he was finally brought to a large room with ribbed vaults overhead. A bench joined to the woodwork extended along the room's four walls. Some fifty people, waiting for rulings on their fate, were talking together in groups.

An hour later the two inspectors came for Bridet. All three got back into the little Simca and a short time later arrived at the Prison de la Santé. En route, while driving along Rue Saint-Jacques, Bridet had glimpsed the house on the corner of Boulévard du Port-Royal where he had once rented a studio after quitting law school and then storming out of the legal department of the insurance company where he worked in order to become a painter.

The gate of the prison, with an entrance built into one of its two doors, wasn't all that imposing. It was almost the entryway of a handsome apartment building on an avenue off the Étoile. Above it floated the French flag, lifeless, soulless despite its bright colors.

Bridet crossed a sort of courtyard roofed over with glass and resembling a cage, what for the metal gates on all sides of it. A guard opened one of these gates. Within a wide gallery strange offices were set in rows, each having its own roof although protected by the glass above.

Bridet was shoved into a room containing no furniture but cluttered with coat racks. Shortly after, a door opened. The Clerk's Office employee who appeared on the threshold wasn't some harmless bureaucrat. He belonged to the penal administration and as such he had not always spent his time shuffling papers.

"Are you prepared to come?"

"Yes, of course," said Bridet.

He was shown into a large room, bare and clean, in which hovered a delightful odor of wood-smoke. It looked like a study hall that has just been swept and tidied and its stove lit. He was requested to empty his pockets. The two inspectors hadn't yet left. One of them went up to Bridet to verify that he had not kept anything on him. He ran his hands over his body, not simply over his pockets but down his legs as well. Then, stepping behind, he started his little routine all over again. Suddenly, brandishing a fistful of papers, he demanded: "And this?"

"What's that?" asked Bridet.

"That's what I am asking you."

"I don't know."

The inspector brought the papers over to his colleague who distributed some to the Clerk's Office staff.

"These are leaflets," said one of them.

"Leaflets?" exclaimed Bridet.

"No, pictures of the Blessed Virgin," quipped the inspector with the prettily drawn nose.

He turned toward Bridet and, switching to the familiar *tu* for the first time, said: "You hadn't mentioned that you were a communist . . ."

Bridet kept his mouth closed. Had his freedom not been at stake he would have answered out of defiance that he was one.

"You aren't about to tell me these leaflets fell out of the sky!"

Bridet still maintained his silence.

"While you're at it, why not say that we're the ones who stuck them in your pocket."

"I'm not accusing anyone."

Everybody passed the leaflets back and forth, ostentatiously holding them between the tips of their fingers as though the paper were unclean, not daring to keep them too long for fear of appearing to be interested in what was printed on them.

"This is Thorez's manifesto," said one bureaucrat.

"That fellow, eh!" exclaimed another.

"Listen to this, you just won't believe your ears," cried out a scrivener who had remained behind his table and seemed to have a reputation for being a deadpan humorist: " 'France wants to live free and independent. Never shall a people like ours be a nation of slaves. It is in the people that the great hopes for national and social liberation reside. The freedom front will form itself around the ardent and generous working class.' "

"Don't go reading us that crap all the way through!" angrily interrupted the inspector with the finely chiseled features.

The scrivener, who had no doubt tried to be witty (unless he had not been loath to voice one or two truths) fell silent immediately. He looked at his colleagues the way, back in the world, a husband looks at his wife. Those colleagues averted their eyes. Wit as practiced among the Penal Authorities did not seem the same as that found among the police.

"You think you can set me up!" yelled Bridet. "But it isn't going to work!"

"Shut your mouth!"

"Look me in the eye," continued Bridet just as loudly. "You know damned well that you stuck them in my pocket, you know damned well you did, and if you say you didn't you're a filthy liar."

The inspector started shouting in turn. A fact was a fact. He wasn't going into any of the details. Bridet turned toward the onlookers.

"All right, you were here, you saw everything. You know I didn't have any leaflets on me. And you let this go on, and you say nothing. You should feel ashamed."

There was a moment of embarrassment. Then murmurings arose.

"That's enough, we're getting fed up with this, we really are, you know, so stop acting so smart. All right? You go on that way any longer and you're going to pay for it. We want to treat you nice, but don't take us for a bunch of fools, you can explain it all to the judge, we've got our job to do, that's what we're doing, and that's all there is to it."

At this juncture the head warden entered the room, wearing the dark prison staff uniform whose stripes instead of gilded are a dull shade of blue. His mustache ended in twists and his hair was tousled. For fun he clicked his heels and gave a Hitler salute. However it may have been meant as a joke you sensed in him a vague regret that it wasn't the French salute. That clicking of the heels and that outflung arm, how much more of an effect they made than an open hand at the visor of a cap.

"You're not in Berlin!" shouted the inspector, pouncing on this distraction.

"So what do we do?" one of the Clerk's Office staff asked a moment later.

"The report, there's got to be the report. You can see we've got to get through with that if we're ever going to be able to get out of here," said the inspector.

"Is it really worth the bother?"

"Damned right it's worth the bother."

The clerks glanced at each other. To be mixed up in this business obviously repelled them. But as the inspector kept insisting, they began to fear that they might be suspected of having a secret sympathy for communists.

And so the report was drawn up.

In the cell in section B there were already three prisoners: a truck driver who had driven up onto a sidewalk and crushed an eight-year-old girl and an old woman against a wall. A Pole who had killed one of his compatriots, in self-defense, he claimed. And finally a dubious character whom German soldiers had brought to a police station on Rue Rochechouart. They had seen him extorting money from women of ill-repute in a brothel, threatening them with a knife. The French police had thanked those soldiers at length. Given this rare instance where collaboration could not be criticized, they had indulged in it to their heart's content. The chief of the vice squad had even contacted the German authorities to find out what sort of reward would be suitable for those upstanding soldiers.

The three prisoners welcomed Bridet very cordially. The time they had spent in prison made this one seem less awful to them. To their mind Bridet was taking an overly tragic view of what had befallen him. The first day was the worst. They could assure him that by tomorrow he would already be feeling better.

Bridet dropped down onto the stool. When they had shoved him into the cell he, greatly aroused, had let out a shout, begun to wriggle backwards. And now, a few minutes later, here he sat, suddenly sundered from the world, without knowing why or for how long. He thought about the leaflet business. They'd certainly wanted to worsen his case. But just who had wanted to? Since all it took was an order from the minister for somebody to be arrested, what had been the point of that make-believe? Perhaps he had treated those inspectors too loftily. They had avenged themselves. Yolande too had been maladroit. What need had she to talk about General Stulpnagel's qualities to people who, from the patriotic standpoint, must not have had very clear consciences? Yolande was really too foolish. But at the thought that she was perhaps weeping at this very moment, his heart softened.

As the inspectors were leading him away she had said to him: "Tonight you'll be free." The whole day long Bridet believed that she was going to come and get him, that he would at least have news of her. But the rhythm of his existence had abruptly changed. One day, two days, three days are mere minutes in the life of prisons. And a week elapsed before he saw Yolande again. He was so demoralized that upon finding himself in her presence, before she could even utter a word, he had wrapped his

arms around her, for a long time hugged her to him without speaking, as if freedom had now ranked in importance
after the happiness of seeing her again. She extricated
herself as soon as she could decently do so.

"You're free!" she said to him, opening her eyes wide
to give her face a look of candor.

"What!"

"Yes, you're free."

Bridet took her by the shoulders again and again, in his
joy gave her not one long lingering kiss, but pecked hur-
riedly at all the parts of her face.

"Come, come now, darling, let me tell you what happened."

She had gone to see Outhenin at the Préfecture de Police. She had acquainted him with the latest developments. He had appeared profoundly surprised. He told her
to come back, that he was going to inquire around the
departments. The minister must surely have been inex-
actly informed. The decision he had taken must have been
based on a report established previously. Through some
regrettable oversight, excusable nevertheless in a period
of reorganization, the results of the investigation had no
doubt not been communicated to him.

Two days later she had seen Outhenin again. He had
read aloud to her the telegram he had sent to Vichy. He
was awaiting an answer. Yolande had gone back again the
next day. Right off the bat Outhenin had announced the
good news to her: the nullifying of the minister's decision. All that remained was to notify the departments
concerned. That would take two or three days at the outside. She hadn't waited for everything to be settled before
coming to see him. She knew only too well what it meant
to be in a state of uncertainty.

"But has the prosecutor been advised?"

"What prosecutor?"

"The fact is that I'm charged with conspiring against the internal security of the State. The police have nothing more to do with my case. I'm in the hands of the law. Didn't Outhenin speak to you about it?"

"Why the law?"

"Because of the communist leaflets."

"What leaflets?"

"The ones they planted in my pocket."

Yolande gazed at her husband a long while.

"So you had leaflets?"

"No, of course I didn't!" shouted Bridet. "Those bastard cops stuck them in my pocket."

Yolande smiled skeptically.

"That strikes me as rather extraordinary," she said.

"It's true nevertheless. You don't believe me?"

"Yes, I do, but this sort of story has always seemed extraordinary to me. Why would you have people stick leaflets in your pocket? When it's known that someone is a highway robber and when proof of it is lacking, I can understand. But that's not the case with you. The police had a proper warrant."

"Ah! You've got some odd ideas. You call that proper, do you."

Yolande kept silent a moment.

"Do you swear to me it's true?" she asked.

A certain helpless confusion was visible on her face. This story seemed unbelievable, but she couldn't doubt her husband.

"If what you're telling me is true," she added, "it's going to cause an outcry."

She had a sorrowful expression on her face. She was basically very good-hearted and the revelation of such abominable doings shook her composure. She started to mull things over. It was bewildering to her that they would have acted this way with her husband. For the first time a doubt entered her mind about the trustworthiness of Outhenin and all her Vichy friends. But when we believe in people it is never all at once that we withdraw our confidence in them. She was in the presence of some tricky legal maneuver. They had realized they had made a blunder. They had concocted this business in order to get the case shifted from one department to another. At the same time those leaflets were being placed in her husband's pocket, the Minister of Justice was being notified. Bridet would be acquitted and there would be no need for the Ministry of the Interior to issue a retraction.

"I'm going to talk about all of this with Outhenin," said Yolande. "He simply has to give me the final word on the matter."

"And if there's a final word at all, it's that your Outhenin engineered the thing," said Bridet.

Yolande did not reply. She gave her husband a lingering kiss. Then as she took leave of him she said, in order to comfort him, that such deeds always backfire against their perpetrators.

CHAPTER 16

A few days later Bridet was taken to the Palais de Justice. The examining magistrate impressed him favorably right away. He was much more acute, much more straightforward and much more understanding than all those Vichy functionaries and, yet more emphatically, than all the riffraff Bridet had been dealing with recently. This magistrate looked to be in his fifties. There was a certain carelessness about his appearance. He had the troubled face of a man who over the course of his life has asked himself many questions relating to the moral and sentimental spheres. From his gaze one felt that he saw the human beings who came before him, that he did truly see them and that he judged them not by the behavior that had landed them in court but according to their underlying worth.

He started in upon Bridet's pre-trial examination. The judge told him that he was charged with conspiring against the internal security of the State. He asked him to choose a lawyer, and did so without appearing to consider that the defendant was guilty. Then he asked him to retire. Bridet, who had been waiting for the judge's questions in order to open his heart, stayed put. "You may retire," the judge repeated.

"It's truly unbelievable," exclaimed Bridet, "that such means can be resorted to, that one can construct an accusation upon some low-down police frame-up. I tell you, your Honor, those leaflets were put into my pocket by a policeman. I'd already heard of such things but I'd never wanted to believe them. You have to be the personal victim of them. Yes, I tell you they were put into my pocket. Such a thing is dishonoring to the law. Before the war that used to be done with cocaine, cocaine was planted in the pockets of bullies or pimps. Nowadays anybody at all can be treated this way . . .

"Please, please," said the judge gently.

He lifted his arms in a weary gesture and seemed to be saying, Bridet felt, that the defendant was putting himself to much unnecessary trouble, for as yet there was no indication that he had been charged with anything. He had been inculpated, it was true, but under the present circumstances that was unlikely to lead to any consequence other than a few trifling personal annoyances that would soon pass; and to defend oneself with such vehemence pointed to a certain shallowness of mind, for all men, these days, be they judges or culprits, employers or workers, were in the same boat.

Once back in his cell Bridet had the comforting feeling that the Boches had not contaminated everything, that in certain milieux little vestiges of France still existed.

Yolande came back to see him on Sunday. She was changed. Outhenin had sent her to speak to a certain Jean-Claude Fallières. Her fondness for people of some social standing was such that even in this prison visitors' room she could not prevent herself saying that she thought he was the grandson of the former President of the Republic, which was moreover not so. He hadn't seemed surprised by this leaflet business. In his opinion, everything was possible. Then she had gone over to the Préfecture to try and see Schlessinger. They told her he was on a trip. "But Monsieur Outhenin told me that he was back." She had lost her temper. She had spoken of lodging a complaint with General Glouton. But this threat had made no impression. From the vantage point of Paris there was nothing very fearsome about Vichy, even regarding the services that had remained under Vichy's auspices. She'd gone back to see Outhenin who, in turn, had slipped off. All these people were self-centered and cowardly. They kept a mutual eye on one another. In reality they had no power. Once they sensed there were interests at stake they drew in their horns. This leaflet business made them jittery. Obviously an investigation would have been in order. Perhaps all it amounted to was something dreamt up by some rank-and-file policemen. But there was no being sure. On the other hand, it was difficult to order such an investigation without appearing to exert pressure on the judiciary, without casting discredit upon the police. And in times like these, the mere fact that one could be suspected of having such an ulterior motive could have far-reaching consequences.

That was when Yolande made up her mind to go over to Avenue Kléber, to the headquarters of General Stulpnagel. Ah! you had to see the difference for yourself! She was shown in right away, without waiting one minute, not by General Stulpnagel, for he was out of town (which was true, the Germans didn't lie), but by another general just as important. All her statements were immediately taken down. An interesting detail was that the German general, perceiving that Yolande's emotional state was preventing her from talking, rose, went over to where she was sitting bolt upright in her armchair and taking her very tactfully by the shoulders obliged her to lean back and make herself comfortable—his gesture was so fatherly tears nearly came to her eyes.

"This is another of those Carlton elevator stories," muttered Bridet. Anyway, after she'd been calmed down and had told him what had happened, he had made no promises, he had given out no hint of what his thoughts were, but she had sensed how very disgusted he had been by the disgraceful procedures she had brought to his attention. On showing her out he shook her hand very firmly and he had looked into her eyes for some time. He had pronounced only a few words, and those words were: "Madame, I shall see what there is for us to do."

During this tale Bridet had to battle to control his temper. When a person is as far from other people as he was from Yolande at that moment, to speak is to widen the already existing gap. There was nothing to do. Nevertheless he said, assuming the most deceptive, the gentlest tone: "What you've done is very fine, my dearest. Thank you. But, you know, I saw the judge and I believe my case is going to be straightened out. So it's better for you to keep nice and quiet. You'll have plenty of time to go into action later on, my dearest, should things take an unfavorable turn."

On March 15, 1941, Bridet was brought before the court, the Fifth Chambre Correctionnelle. En route from Boulévard Arago to the Palais de Justice, a militiaman wanted to handcuff him. "Nah," said another militiaman, "it's not worth bothering about." But upon their arrival, seeing his captain, the first militiaman went up to Bridet and, blocking his body from view, made as if to remove handcuffs from his wrists.

The presiding judge of the Fifth Chamber was a man in his sixties with closely cropped white hair. About him

there was something firm which contrasted with the flab-
biness of his assessors.

Upon entering, Bridet fixed his gaze on the bench, then
on the state prosecutor who, it must be said, looked human enough, capable of a theatrical dropping of charges.
Bridet's lawyer stood up at that moment, and lifting his
arm over the edge of the dock, motioned for his client to
bend towards him. He spoke to Bridet under his breath,
but Bridet wasn't listening. He had caught sight of Yolande. He waved to her. She responded with gestures to
the effect that everything was going fine. Bridet sat down,
very calm. He knew that, for the times, his sentence
wasn't likely to be heavy: at most five years, which he
wouldn't serve out if the war came to an end first. But
that end of the war seemed so far away that he was de-
spondent nevertheless. Basically, his whole life was hanging on this sentence, for however moderate it might be,
no life is more tenuous than the one a man leads behind
bars when the outside world is in upheaval.

The trial lasted a few minutes. To the questions put to
him Bridet answered without hesitation and without anger, for too much time had elapsed since the leaflets had
been placed in his pocket. He had taken on the tone of a
man who doesn't see what the authorities have against
him. He enjoyed some small instances of consideration.
Thus, during the testimony of a false witness (a self-styled
licensed shopkeeper on Rue Demours whom Bridet had
supposedly encouraged to join the communist party and
to whom he had supposedly given leaflets) the judge,
while listening to this peculiar witness' contradictions,
had looked at Bridet and given him an inadvertent wink.

The prosecutor stood up, spouted awful clichés about
the maintaining of law and order and the Bolshevik peril,
then sat down.

[155]

The three judges exchanged a few words. Bridet had the impression that they were favorably inclined toward him. The presiding judge said: "I think it would be wise for you to acknowledge the facts. The court will appreciate this and will show indulgence."

The sentence was at last handed down. The court decided that the facts were not established. Bridet was acquitted by benefit of doubt.

"You are free," said the presiding judge.

"Thank you, thank you, your honor," Bridet said, his face beaming.

It came to him a little later that he had had no reason to thank anybody at all. "Oh, out of graciousness, yes. A little gratitude, a little deference costs so little and gives people such pleasure."

"See you in a minute, wait for me at the exit," he shouted, turning toward Yolande who, on her feet, was waving her arms around to display her joy.

Bridet had already resumed the easy manners of a free man. On leaving the dock, when the militiaman stood back to allow him to walk out first, Bridet placed a friendly hand on his shoulder and said: "No, no, after you . . . your turn now . . ."

As he was getting back into the prison van that would take him to La Santé for his official release, he was able to exchange a few words with Yolande. "You see, you see . . ." she kept saying. "Yes, darling, I've seen . . ."

The formalities were conducted pursuant to the usual rules. Bridet felt they were interminable. At last he signed his name in a big book. Shutting the book, the clerk announced with an air of self-importance: "You are free." Bridet was given back his tie, his shoelaces, the little money he had had on him.

But for the crumpling his clothes had got in the steaming-vat he might have believed he had never even been a prisoner. A guard accompanied him to the first gate. In the glass-roofed courtyard that had to be crossed before reaching the exit stood several groups of people, no doubt new prisoners being brought in. Suddenly two men advanced toward Bridet.

"You are Monsieur Bridet?"

"Yes, why?"

"We've been ordered to take you to the Prefecture. Please come with us."

"Why? How can that be? Why?"

"We don't know anything about it. They'll tell you over there."

While parleying Bridet finally grasped what was going on. At the request of the German occupation authorities, the Prefect of Police had seen himself obliged to issue an order calling for Bridet's internment. The two inspectors, who moreover looked very uncomfortable about their assignment, explained to him that this often happened when the Germans weren't satisfied with a verdict. They thought that Bridet would be taken to the camp at Venoix, in the Oise, "One of the best," they added.

Bridet's disappointment was so great that he could no longer contain himself.

". . . You call yourselves Frenchmen and you perform such a job for the Boches . . . You are shameless. I'd rather sweep the streets if I needed to earn a living."

At that moment a man separated himself from one of the groups stationed in the courtyard. He was very tall but thin and stooped. His chest was so sunken that one might have thought that he was doubling over as the result of a blow. He was unshaven. He was wearing a dusty bowler hat of no longer stylish shape. He came over and stood in front of Bridet.

"What are you saying?"

Right away Bridet had the impression that this was one of the policemen who were accompanying the new arrivals.

"I am saying that the French who serve the Boches as you are doing at this very moment are traitors and that the day is coming when they will all be shot."

The man took off his hat as though he wanted to put himself on the same level as his interlocutor.

"Are you saying those things to me?" he asked with a strong working class accent.

"To you and to the others."

"Well then, shut your damned mouth. I'm talking to you man to man, you hear me? You've got no right to reproach those who are for the Boches. Me, I'm for the Boches, I'm not hiding it from you. We're all for the Boches, aren't we, gentlemen?"

The two inspectors kept silent, but did not protest.

"When you've done what we've done—you hear me, you pretentious little bastard?—all that's left for you to do is keep your trap shut. That's absolutely right, long live the Boches, they're number one and we're a bunch of ass-holes . . ."

As he picked up further steam the two inspectors moved off. On the way out they endeavored to get at Bridet by way of sentiment. He oughtn't to have talked about France as he had. When you generalize you are always unfair. Then they came out with something that simply astounded Bridet: "The guy back there, he's somebody we know. He's a good guy."

Bridet spent the night and the following day at the Prefecture. He had got word to Yolande, but he was unable to see her because, being continually marched from one office to another, from one floor to another, from one building to another, he had always just left each time she picked up his traces.

Two days later he was interned, as the inspectors had intimated, in the Venoix camp, near Clermont in the Oise.

CHAPTER 17

The Venoix camp looked like a housing development. It had been set up in large concrete pavilions intended for an aviation school whose construction had been interrupted by the war. They were spread out over a vast quadrilateral area. From certain details one could surmise that upon completion they might have been comfortable. Provisions had been made for conveniences unthought of in the past.

This camp's regimen differed so greatly from the prison's that during the first days Bridet felt relieved. The simple fresh air, after leaving the cramped crowded cell at La Santé, seemed an immense boon. The internees had some breathing room. They washed their clothes, boiled water. They took strolls between the pavilions. As companions Bridet found them more agreeable than his former jailmates. They had no crimes on their consciences. You could tell it from their faces, from their easy manner in answering the militiamen, from their surprise before certain penitentiary measures.

Ever since arriving at Venoix, Bridet had been wondering whether Yolande hadn't once again been at the origin of his newest troubles. Had it not been for her going to see the Germans they mightn't perhaps have paid any attention to him. But since other internees, on whose behalf no one had intervened, also wound up here in the aftermath of adventures of a sort almost identical to his, it was probable that she had not influenced his fate in any way.

In the evening hours, when after having questioned the people around him he had got a better grasp of what had happened to him, he wrote at length to Yolande to guide her in the steps she would have to take to obtain his release. The Germans exerted no pressure on the courts but when they esteemed that a court had not fulfilled its duty, that the released individual was dangerous, they would contact the French authorities. This had certainly occurred. A simple note to the chief of police asking for assurances had brought on his internment. Consequently Yolande should proceed with utmost caution. He advised her not to call on her Vichy friends anymore. They had spent too much time over him to have any interest left in this business. Moreover, they had had nothing to do with it, and were they to intervene—supposing that were possible—it would most likely be to his detriment. It was better to leave the Vichyite police out of the picture, even if they were well-intentioned, and to try to approach some figure who was playing an important role in the relations between the new French government and the German occupation authorities.

Bridet had spent three weeks in the camp before Yolande finally obtained authorization to see him. Her visit did him much good. He had been expecting that his wife would appear before him swollen-eyed and contrite, conscious of being in some measure responsible for what had befallen him, and seeking his forgiveness. He had dreaded this for, given his low spirits, what he had need of was not wringing of hands and regrets, but cheerfulness and con-

who even inspire their respect, and whom it is in the Germans' interest to treat with consideration? It's the army."

Yolande should have thought of this earlier, in Vichy for example, instead of wasting her time running between the Hotel du Parc and the Célestins. She should not have bothered to go anywhere except to the Ministry of War. But it wasn't too late. If the prefects didn't bestir themselves, well then she'd turn in that direction.

"Be careful," Bridet told her.

A month passed during which Bridet did not hear from his wife. She had surely been writing to him, but the letters must have been impounded somewhere. The idea of escaping recurred to him more and more often. He had the impression that the longer he waited the more difficult it would be for him to join de Gaulle. The police were getting organized. And, too, a disturbing rumor was starting to go around the camp. The prisoners they took away in the wake of those visits from German officers, they weren't taken away to be tried. They were hostages. And if nobody heard anything more about them, the reason was very simple. They had been shot.

When Yolande did finally come back to see her husband he advised her of his intention to escape. She made no answer, not daring to dissuade him, but when he asked for her help she remarked that it was truly pointless to take such a risk just as he was about to be freed. From Wiesbaden she had received a letter from an officer at General Huntziger's staff headquarters, a Captain Aloysius Dupont, delegate to the Armistice Commission. He had seen to it that the steps she desired had been taken. According to the information he had been able to obtain and which he was pleased to communicate to her, they knew about her husband's case. Monsieur Joseph Bridet was in absolutely no danger. He was being held at the Venoix camp not because of the gravity of his acts, but in consequence of our former adversaries' obligation toward the French population not to go back on a decision they had taken. One could however envisage that in the very near future a solution satisfactory to all concerned would be adopted. Schlessinger, for his part, had gathered the same information. "I must tell you something else that you'll be glad to hear," Yolande added. "Since you've been in the camp, everybody's attitude has completely changed toward you. Our friends' kindness and obligingness have deeply moved me. Even Outhenin is doing everything he can for you, and with utmost sincerity. You know, for all the squabbling we French do among ourselves, there's one thing that immediately turns us back into friends, and that's foreigners taking it into their heads to meddle in our affairs."

A few days later Bidet was summoned to the camp director's office. Captain Lepelletier looked like a decent sort. He didn't even raise his eyes to look at Bridet. He announced that the Minister of the Interior had asked him for a report on Bridet's conduct.

"Here's the report I made on you," added the captain, holding it out to Bridet and inviting him to read it.

It was a banal report, mainly containing dates. It concluded with the following neutral sentence: "Joseph Bridet's conduct has provided grounds for no remarks in particular."

After he had handed back the report, Bridet, not knowing why he had been made to read it, kept silent, waiting for some sort of question. But the captain asked him none at all. Still without lifting his head, he told him he could go.

"Why did you have me read that report?" Bridet asked.
"For your guidance, for your guidance . . ."

For the rest of the day Bridet thought no more about this incident. But once in bed he suddenly remembered it.

It was odd. Since when did a camp director have the party concerned read the report that he was sending to his superior? It was plainly a piece of kindness. But Bridet didn't know this captain. So why this kindness? There was obviously some implication that Bridet was expected to understand. It was a little as if Lepelletier, in the event something were to happen, had wanted to relieve himself of any responsibility. That was one interpretation. Another more reassuring one was that, suspecting that the prisoner was about to be freed, this captain had wanted to win his sympathy. How was one to know the truth? Bridet finally fell asleep.

During the weeks that ensued Bridet heard nothing more of this report. He finally ceased thinking about it. This request for information had undoubtedly resulted once again from that need on the part of the administration, eager to keep the upper hand wherever it could, to act authoritatively.

Bridet was becoming used to life in the camp. He had become close to a few of his companions. They all had more or less the same way of feeling and reacting to things. Psychologically speaking, he was less alone than when he had been free. These two hundred and fifty men, coming from the most varied social backgrounds, commanded respect through their unity. They gave an impression of strength and Bridet, just as he did in the buffet at the station after crossing the Demarcation Line, felt proud to belong to such a group of men. Within it he felt sheltered, much more so than in the corridors of the Vichyite ministries. Nothing could be done to hurt him him. He was a member of a collectivity that was big enough to respond to any measure taken against it. Several times already the authorities had been obliged to revoke a decision.

However, one evening the rumor spread through the camp that two internees, transferred three days before to the prison in Clermont, had been executed. Their names were given. Some maintained that they had been guillotined, which seemed so monstrous to Bridet that he did not believe it. To his mind such horror stories still belonged to the world of the imagination. Moreover, among his comrades a good many shared his skepticism. But there were others, just as numerous, who were convinced of the rumor's truth. "If it's true, then it's because our two friends committed acts we don't know about," Bridet remarked. "Not at all," came the reply. "They did nothing at all. They were executed as hostages." One was a fifty-seven-year-old man from a very modest station in life (he was a manual laborer who had had the misfortune to be a member of a workingmen's organization); he had been interned for making disparaging remarks about the Chief of State in the days following Montoire.* Taking advantage of the friendly feelings of a camp employee whom he had won over by recounting how he had once written for the newspapers, Bridet sought to discover the truth. Two men had indeed been executed. But he wasn't able to find out anything further. Nonetheless, he did get the impression that in the camp office they had known a week in advance that the two men were going to be exe-

---

* Montoire-sur-Loir, a small village near Tours, site of the meeting between Hitler and Marshal Pétain on October 24, 1940, publicly dramatizing the policy of collaboration between Nazi Germany and Vichy France. (Translator's note.)

[167]

cuted (the second was a twenty-seven-year-old school teacher). Thus while the prisoners were doing their laundry, writing to their families, engaging in all the little activities that helped pass the time, these functionaries had known that two men were going to be put to death. That they had gone right on watching over the camp as if everything were normal made them odious overnight. Altercations broke out between the guards and the internees. Captain Lepelletier contemplated stern measures. In the end, some functionaries were transferred. Calm was restored. But the atmosphere remained charged even so. Not a day went by without a rumor going round that other hostages were about to be picked out. Newspapers made their way into the camp. With each report of an armed attack or act of sabotage a great restlessness manifested itself. Groups formed outside the administration buildings. The camp authorities were finally roused to action. It was then that they posted the declaration whose main lines were as follows: "The authorities have noted a certain agitation resulting from the presumed designation of hostages. They wish hereby to inform the internees of the Venoix camp that the government of the French State is opposed to any designating of hostages in the internment camps, that any rumors which have gone about on this subject are groundless, that no hostage has ever been designated, let alone executed."

This declaration calmed certain spirits, but left Bridet absolutely indifferent. To the government of the French State, so touchy where it was a question of honor and rectitude, one lie more or one lie less didn't matter. All it took was assurances from the State that certain categories of the French population would not be affcted for those certain categories of the French population to be instantly on guard.

Bridet wrote to Yolande that he wanted to see her right away. Using indirect language he indicated to her what was going on. This feeling of being at the mercy of a chance designation made camp life very hard. She answered that he shouldn't allow himself to be carried away by impressions like this. She was busy on his behalf. She was in hope of seeing things reach a conclusion shortly. In two weeks at the most she would come and see him, and she would come not empty-handed, but with a piece of good news.

True to her promise, two weeks later she arrived in the camp. Including the time spent in La Santé, that made nearly six months since Bridet had ceased to be a free man. He had grown very thin. It wouldn't have mattered except for the feeling he had of being caught in a vise that was tightening inexorably. Despite the initiatives she had taken, her comings and goings, her letters, her appeals to friendship, he was still a prisoner and under conditions which were worsening by slow degrees. When he caught sight of his wife, hardly changed, actually looking better than ever, visibly happy at having resumed an active life, he got the impression not that she had shed her ties with him, but that she didn't realize the gravity of the situation. She kissed him like a woman reunited with a warrior, pretending to forget that she was stylishly dressed and carefully made-up. She told him right away that if she hadn't come earlier it was because she had been waiting for a big piece of news. She had just received it. Bridet was free. It was over. He was no longer a prisoner . . .

For a moment Bridet remained mute with joy. "Ah, my darling," he exclaimed at last, "if you only knew the weight you've lifted from me!" He explained that he hadn't suffered from life in the camp. He hadn't cared about eating badly, about sleeping badly, about living in a building whose concrete was not yet dry. He had never attached any importance to his comforts. Yolande knew this was true. What had been awful was wondering each morning whether hostages had been designated, whether he was going to be among them.

With the coming of evening Bridet started to regret that he hadn't asked Yolande for more specific details. This was often what happened with good news. Out of fear of discovering a not so good side to it, one dares not talk about it. He was set free, but for the time being here he still was. "She'd meant," thought Bridet, "that my release was signed, that legally I was free. But I have to wait for the formalities to be completed."

A week went by without bringing him the slightest news concerning his release. Rumors of all sorts were still rife in the camp. Some faded out the way they had arisen, but others persisted, swelling with contradictory reports. Among these rumors there was one which constantly recurred under different guises. A high officer, some even said a general, had been assassinated nearby, in Beauvais. Another also had been killed, even closer, in Clermont, unless it was the same person. The inhabitants of those two towns had been confined to their homes. More, they had been strictly enjoined not to lock their doors at night. When you considered what they were having to put up with, the Venoix internees could almost be thought of as lucky. "You're going to see what they're in for," some were saying. There is no situation more fraught with menace than that of prisoners who, thanks to an extraordinary combination of circumstances, find themselves better off than the population at large.

Bridet sought reassurance in the thought that if hostages were designated, he wouldn't be among them since the camp authorities, even though they hadn't executed the order to release him, had certainly received it. This assumption did not satisfy him, however. If they were to disregard the order, what would he be able to do? He had already encountered this in Vichy. Even if they had made a mistake, the authorities would not acknowledge it. The designation of a hostage is not something that can be revoked, it is far too serious a matter to allow of that, especially in as much as the removal of one name from the list implies the designating of another to replace it.

A few more days passed without the prisoners hearing anything new. There was even one entire day during which no mention was made of the German officer that had been killed. But the same rumors suddenly started going around again, with many more details than before. In Clermont, during the same night, a German colonel and a private had been assassinated. If the culprits didn't turn themselves in within twenty-four hours, fifteen hostages would be designated and shot.

This news made such an impression on Bridet that he felt filled by a wild anger against Yolande. He needed to attack somebody. That woman was truly a criminal. She was to blame for his being here. Why, since she claimed that he had been freed, why hadn't she done anything on his behalf, why hadn't she got them to move along with the formalities? He hadn't hidden it from her that he was in danger, had he? He set to writing her a letter on the spot, but couched it in such strong language that he didn't dare entrust it to the mail clerk. Coincidentally a certain Baumé, more fortunate than Bridet, since someone at least was bestirring himself in his behalf, was supposed to leave the camp that very evening. Bridet handed him the letter he had written. He asked him to go and see Yolande, to talk with her, tell her what was going on. Listening to her husband through the intermediary of a stranger she would be more accessible.

The afternoon seemed endless. Every conversation revolved around this designation of hostages. If fifteen were taken that meant that each man stood about one chance in twenty of being included in the group. Around five o'clock he had the occasion to share a bottle of wine with a friend. Wasn't there an element of exaggeration in all these rumors? It wasn't so very long ago when the camp authorities had declared that there would never be any picking of hostages. They couldn't have gone back on their word all that fast. And anyway, could they be so sure this officer had been killed on account of his being a German? According to certain gossip he had been killed by the husband of a woman who had caught him in the act in his own house. In reality it was a crime of passion. They couldn't shoot fifteen men because a husband had killed his wife's lover. As for the soldier, he had been drunk. It was on the morning after a brawl between German soldiers that his body was found in front of the Alcazar.

Bridet stretched out on his bed. All his barrack mates were there. Normally this was card-playing time, but this evening all they did was talk. Bridet would have liked to be alone, not to see anybody. He still didn't believe hostages would be designated, but neither in 1939 had he believed there'd be a war. He lay with his hands behind his head. One can't shut one's ears the way one shuts one's eyes. It hurt having to hear incessantly repeated what he had heard the whole day long. What is most oppressive in life's tragic moments is the disarray of those around us. Here we've succeeded through an act of will in driving from our minds everything apt to incline us to fear, only to find ourselves surrounded by people who haven't made the effort we have. Bridet couldn't bear hearing them talk anymore. He went outside to be by himself behind a building. A half-hour later, as he was coming back, he ran into Baumé. "I'm not going," Baumé said, giving his letter back to Bridet. Baumé was pale. His hands were shaking a little. He had just been told that his departure had been put off.

The news made such an impact upon Bridet that, some minutes later, when he looked for his letter, he wasn't able to find it at first. He had folded it in half and then folded it in half again and tucked it deep into his pocket. The stranglehold was tightening. If they suspended the departure of a man whose papers were all ready, how could Bridet still count on being released? Orders were plainly coming in from outside. Captain Lepelletier and his lieutenants merely had the job of carrying them out.

But a great shock such as this enlightens us. When we feel that our lives can be taken from us, we turn and look inward and we realize that there is only one thing capable of making us strong enough to face this ordeal, and it is to act in strict accordance with our conscience. That evening, in bed, Bridet was overcome with shame for all he had said and hoped for that day. He had said that the German colonel had been killed by a jealous husband. But deep in his heart, had his own life not been at stake, he knew very well that he wouldn't have wanted it that way. On the contrary, he would have maintained that that Boche had been deliberately killed by a patriot and that every last Boche should be killed. He had hoped for his release. What cowardice! At a moment when Frenchmen were about to die, he himself would have been willing to leave, he would have abandoned his fellow countrymen.

Towards nine o'clock in the morning it was learned that officers from the Kommandantur at Beauvais had called upon the camp authorities at a very early hour.

[173]

They had had a civilian with them. He was reported to have been the secretary-general of the sub-prefecture in Clermont. To him the administrators of the camp had turned over more than one hundred and eighty files. Those files were now sitting over at the Ministry of the Interior.

These rumors plunged Bridet into a state of profound dejection. He didn't want to believe them. They were just idle talk. How had all that come to be known? Assuming it was true, how had the prisoners found out about it two hours later? Bridet had some ironic thoughts about the always well-informed sort of people. But that delegation or whatever it could be called had been seen by numerous fellow internees. If its reason for coming was unknown, there was no denying that it had in fact come. Bridet answered that it was altogether natural for the Germans to visit the camps. They were occupying the country. In their capacity of occupyers they went everywhere. As for the rest, it was mere conjecture.

Nothing worthy of note transpired during the course of the day. On the following day Bridet wrote another, much shorter letter to Yolande. He was glad the first one had not been posted. The weather was splendid. His feeling was that the danger had passed. It had lasted too long to maintain its edge.

Around ten o'clock Bridet was looking out the window situated directly above his bed when all of a sudden, on the road beyond the barbed wire, he made out two trucks inside which men were standing. The distance was still too great to see just who those men were. The trucks were approaching, leaving in their wake a cloud of dust that billowed along the road. Then he recognized them as German soldiers. They were coming to relieve the French militia. Bridet, who, in the normal course of life, had always kept bad news to himself, was so struck that he at once called out to his mates. They crowded together at the windows. For a few minutes they did not appear to grasp the import of this changing of the guards. Then, as if there was relief to be found in blackening the situation further, they burst out in lamentations. It wasn't fifteen hostages they were going to shoot, but thirty, fifty. And the Boches wouldn't bother to inquire whether or not these men were married, were fathers, were the mainstays of families, were heroes from the other war, maimed veterans, and so on.

Bridet regretted having thrown the barracks into a tumult. As he tried to explain to his mates that all was not lost, their fierce replies reduced him to silence. Bridet was blind. He imagined, did he, that the Boches had made the trip to the camp for the fun of it? Ah, he was going to see. It wouldn't be long. He'd know what was what pretty damned soon. But this collective anger very quickly subsided.

"We've really got to try to get some idea of what's going on," said one of the internees.

"One of us ought to go over to the office and find out," suggested another.

Bridet volunteered. A short time later he asked Lieutenant Corsetti whether it was true that hostages were going to be taken in the camp. Scarcely had he got the question out than the lieutenant started waving his arms about like a madman. "But you're out of your senses! What's gotten into all of you? Have you already forgotten that we put out a statement? It's incredible that some men can be so nervous. There must certainly be some agitators stirring you all up. What sort of opinion are you going to give to the Germans who've got an eye on us?

We've already got the reputation for being excitable and unreliable, now they're going to think we're a pack of yellow-bellies."

The militiamen having been replaced by the Germans and nothing having happened, calm and hope returned. The new guards were observed, but no one approached them yet. They didn't act in a threatening way. And what was reassuring was that you felt they blindly did what they were told and wouldn't do anything on their own. But in the middle of the night, at different times, isolated shots rang out. There was a tenseness in the air. It all felt as if the orders they were under were so strict that the sentries were cutting loose at every shadow they saw.

During the course of the following morning the internees sought to question the sentries. These, at first, behaved in an approachable way. But they must have figured out what the internees were after, for that same afternoon every last one of them acted as if he was ready to use his gun the moment anybody drew near.

It was not until four o'clock that consternation seized the camp once again. A gray-painted German-make car with its top down, after having begun sounding its horn while still a good five hundred yards away so that the orderly on duty at the gate would have time to open it, tore into the camp and screeched to a halt in front of the office building. A high-ranking German officer got out first, followed by a sub-prefect and two lieutenants who were under the captain in command of the camp. Sentries snapped to attention. The officer raised his right arm straight before him, clicked his heels. The sub-prefect had taken off his hat. The lieutenants, a step or so to the rear, stood with their right hand at their caps. You could sense that they were rather proud to be able to go on saluting that way. Under foreign domination though they were, nobody had dared to forbid them to salute in their wonted manner.

Before the renewal of pessimism all about him, Bridet felt himself weaken. His fellow internees believed that something terrible was about to happen; he alone would not let go of hope. He said: "Nothing proves hostages are going to be picked. It could be that they want to put us in a different camp." He was met with stares. But this time the others didn't fly off the handle; they were beginning to understand Bridet's character.

At night, gun shots, more of them this time, rang out anew. Bridet was afraid. There is in the monstrous way a collectivity is managed a seeming need to create a preparatory atmosphere. These pointless gun shots, he now understood, were certainly a kind of necessary warm-up for the performance of an abomination.

At eight o'clock shouts went up in the building. The man whose job was to go for the coffee hadn't been able to get out. A sentry was posted at the door. Everybody gathered at the windows. Bridet, alone, remained seated on his bed. He had suddenly felt overwhelmed by an immense depression and, which was curious, it had come upon him at the very moment when his mates, indignant at being shut in, were instead gesticulating and yelling, protesting violently against a measure which at once prevented them from having water to wash in and coffee to drink. Head in hands, Bridet wasn't listening to them. He was thinking that they were right. Hostages had been designated. That's what they had been telling him, and he, with his determination never to see the bad side, he had not believed them. He reviewed the years of his youth, he watched them go past. How lively they seemed! They belonged to a time that lay far behind him, and yet he had the impression that if he had been free and able to return to where he had spent those years, he would have rediscovered everything in the same place, as though neither time nor the war had existed. Then he thought of Yolande. Never would she receive his letter in time, and even if she did, it would be too late. There was an instant when the idea of somehow fighting back in his own defense entered his mind. He had been told often enough that whatever misfortunes came his way were through his own fault. Since his release order had been signed, why hadn't he spoken to them about it at the office? Why this eternal negligence? He wouldn't have been believed . . . Well then, he would have pounded on the table, would have insisted that they make a phone call, etc. And this very minute, instead of being in danger of death, he would be snugly at home.

It was then he felt someone touching his shoulder. It was the man who had the bed next to his. "Well now, what's wrong with you?" he asked Bridet, who was so surprised he didn't know what to answer. "You won't be among them, not you," continued his neighbor. Bridet then understood that, actually, all was not lost and he blushed with shame at having been so hypocritical in his own regard by blaming himself for the shortcomings that had prevented him from escaping the common fate.

A little over an hour went by. Suddenly there came the sound of voices. Yet again some prisoners rushed to the windows, but at that moment the people whose talk had caught their attention pushed through the door. A group of men, headed by three German officers, entered the pavilion.

"Greetings, gentlemen," said one of the officers, no longer as if he were addressing his country's cowardly enemies, but rather men whom circumstances had suddenly elevated to very high rank.

The Frenchmen accompanying these officers stared fixedly straight ahead. They were concealing their uneasiness, concentrating upon standing still. They looked as if they were accomplishing a duty which their higher consciousness of France's commanding interest forbade anyone to judge.

"Prepare yourself to move over here to my right when your name is called," said one of the Germans, as if addressing men whose courage, however disgraceful their conduct had been, was not subject to doubt.

Since no one had come to attention he added: "Stand at attention." He wanted to give the impending murder an air of coming about in accordance with the normal rules. The prisoners obeyed. Two among them had never been soldiers and did so awkwardly.

"Bouc, Maurice," the Boche officer began.

"Poupet, Raoul.

"Grunbaum, David."

Thereupon an extraordinary incident occurred. After having pronounced the name "Grunbaum," the German turned his head a little to one side and spat on the ground, making a spluttering noise several times, *pfui, pfui,* but in such a way that it was clear to all present that his aim was not to put on a public display of his disgust for Jews, but to protect himself superstitiously from taint.

"De Courcieux, Jean.

"Bridet, Joseph."

A light flashed within Bridet's brain. His name had been spoken, no more; and yet it was all over.

The hostages were taken to a building especially set up to receive them. Others were already inside. They were singing. When the newcomers arrived they broke off and shouted insults at the sentries. The imminence of death had liberated them from all fear. When the door shut again they resumed their singing and the new men joined in. Even though there was a great tightness in his throat Bridet sang too. Soon they stopped. They conferred together in groups. It wasn't possible that they be shot. Captain Lepelletier had put in with the people upstairs. Nobody had seen him for two days. New hope began to take shape. Then this bustle gave way to utter listlessness. No one spoke anymore now. They were all writing. Bridet was the only one not writing. He had no more strength for that than he did for singing. But, in spite of himself, he nevertheless had to do what everybody else was doing.

"My dear Yolande," he began, "I am going to be shot in a little while." He stopped, horrified by what he had just written. A few minutes later, as his neighbors were continuing to write, he started again: "I send you all my love. You know that I loved you a great deal. I would have liked to have seen you again." He slowly traced his words on the paper, the while thinking about Yolande and thinking about what he felt for her. But he saw oncoming death, it was there during every instant, and he was forced to break off. Then he no longer understood why he was writing. "Give my books to my brother when he comes home. You should of course keep the ones you want. Go and see my mother. Don't tell her what happened to me. I send you my love once more, darling. Long live France, and you my dear Yolande, have a happy life."

He started to cry. What he had been saying amounted to so little compared to what he might have said had he not had to die. It did no good that he had loved Yolande more than anything in the world, he could no longer tell her so. He added "I love you, I love you," like a child at the bottom of a letter.

Then he got to his feet, went over to a young redheaded

man who had freckles around his eyes. He had taken an immediate liking to him. This young man was sitting down, hands dangling between his legs, completely indifferent to what was going on. Bridet took one of his hands. This contact had the effect of cool water upon the temples. To be shot like this, while holding this hand, it would be less dreadful. But it would be thought that they were afraid. They would be told that they ought to die like men. Bridet let go of the hand.

At three o'clock the priest from Venoix made his entrance into the camp. He was accompanied by German officers, civilians and a police captain. They walked slowly as if to relieve the execution of any hastiness which could have given it a barbarous color. But one sensed that they were in a hurry and that at bottom they had but one abiding thought: to get this over with as quickly as possible.

At ten minutes past four the hostages were assembled in front of the building. A little farther off a truck was maneuvering so as to head towards the road; it was hampered by another truck whose motor wouldn't start. The Germans bustled about. This small problem seemed to have been enough to make them forget the reason they were here. It took no more than this to rekindle a spark of hope. "Back up," they were told. "Want a helping hand?" one of them called out, striving for a bantering effect, but there was something so tragic in his voice that it appeared to have been lost on everybody.

Bridet was among the hostages, but unobtrusive, like a foreigner, totally inconspicuous next to those who kept breaking out with songs without ever singing anything through to the end, or those who sometimes emerged from the group gesticulating, calling upon human justice, trying to provoke who knows what sort of incident following which they would be reprieved. He was in the back row, but it wasn't like high school or the army anymore. Behind the others though he might be, he wasn't left out.

They proceeded with a roll call. As chance would have it Bridet's name was the last to be pronounced, and the whole time this formality lasted he was able to hope that it wouldn't be called, that at the last moment some judicial incident (the fact that he had been designated as a hostage whereas legally he was no longer supposed to belong in the camp) had occurred.

Despite being helped, it required a physical effort to get up into the truck. Bridet blacked out. His companions hauled him up. The bumpy ride brought him around. The weather was superb. Bridet gazed at the sun, without it hurting his eyes in the least. Was that imminent death? Yet this sun seemed to him to be intensely alive in the blue sky, and its rays lengthened and shortened ceaselessly, like flames.

Bridet thought he would have no more strength for dismounting from the truck than he had had for boarding it. It was then that an extraordinary idea came to him, one of those simple ideas which, depending on how much of ourselves we put into them, seem either inspired or insignificant. It suddenly restored all his strength to him. The idea was that, whatever he might do, he could no longer escape death and that, since die he must, he might as well die bravely.

And that is what he did.

The next morning, the women of Venoix came to lay flowers on the graves. They returned in the evening, then on the following days, in ever growing numbers. Soon the graves disappeared under the flowers. The Germans did not interfere. But as these demonstrations were taking a hostile turn and no longer seemed dictated by remembrance but rather by an intent to provoke, the prefecture issued an order forbidding them. Two policemen were stationed at the cemetery entrance. The women tried to pass through anyway. The guards gently pushed them back, urging calm in a good-natured tone that was not very tactful under such circumstances. "Come along now, my good ladies, don't get yourselves all worked up, come along now, be on your way, don't stand about, you've got better things to do back home." As they remained unmoving a few paces away, one of the two policemen turned toward the cemetery, gazed at the graves with the air of a man powerless in the face of destiny. Then he said: "You see for yourself, it's over with. Nothing you're going to do will change their fate one little bit. Come along now, ladies, go back to your homes." The other policemen added: "It was six whole days ago," and he made a gesture which signified that life goes on.

At that moment one woman stepped out from the crowd. She had a gaunt face, fine blue eyes. She was tall and a trifle stooped. She had a black knitted shawl over her shoulders. She walked up to the two guards. All at once, as if undergoing a fit of hysterics, she waving her fists, hammering at the policemen as though upon a wall. She was stamping her feet at the same time. They tried to restrain her. Then losing all control of herself she clung to their shoulder-belts, to the slings of their rifles, to the chin-straps of their helmets, she scratched them, she kicked them. All the while she shrieked: "Murderers, murderers."

AUTHOR'S NOTE

The papers assembled from here and there by Joseph Bridet's friends after his death are of a relative interest. Nevertheless, in the event there is a new edition of this book we will include them as appendixes.

The list includes the following items:

1. Seven poems written between 1935 and 1939.

2. A few hasty notes written in prison and at widely spaced intervals. Plainly Bridet felt he was living through hours whose memory should be preserved. But whether because of the anxiety gnawing him, whether through lack of interest, he had broken off each time.

3. The newspaper articles his editors authorized him to publish in times past under his by-line. There is one among them which seems to invite moving parallels. It is the one containing an account of a public execution. But for the sake of distinctiveness Bridet had adopted such an artificial style that it's impossible to find one sentence conveying, as may the remarks or writings of those who are no more, any hitherto hidden significance.

4. Two letters from Basson written from London, after Bridet had been shot. They are sprinkled with amical expressions in English. When one is aware of the addressee's deplorable end they leave a disagreeable aftertaste. Basson

[185]

speaks of the dangers he escaped from with a self-confidence, a bravado which grate upon the ear. And what is perhaps even more unpleasant is that at no time does it ever occur to him that something could have befallen his old friend who remained behind in France.

5. A deeply affected letter from Outhenin to Yolande, written a few days after Bridet's death, and which begins as follows: "I've just learned of the awful misfortune that has overtaken . . ."

6. A letter from Yolande to her sister-in-law, Mademoiselle Laveyssère, in which, pretending to find herself before a moral dilemma, she asks whether or not she ought to inform her mother-in-law, Madame Bridet, despite her husband's express wish to the contrary.

7. A letter from Madame Bridet to Yolande. This letter from an unhappy old woman, to whom the tragic death of her son has just been announced, is extraordinary. Madame Bridet manifests no surprise, no despair. She speaks of her son as of a stranger and, abruptly, at the end, she asks that he be avenged.

8. The letter the reader already knows of, written by Bridet to his wife before dying, but, prior to being transmitted to her, having been rendered official by French and German stamps and seals as if the authors of his assassination had of course acted within the most perfect legality.

9. A note, dated January 15th, 1941, written in pencil by the Minister of the Interior on that ministry's letterhead, which came into Yolande's possession under rather mysterious circumstances, some three months after the execution of her husband. This note was addressed to Monsieur Saussier. It requests that the Bridet case be shelved indefinitely. The words "shelved indefinitely" are underlined. This note had been dropped off with the Rue

Demours concierge, without explanation, by a stranger to whom no one had paid any attention.

10. A letter emanating from a German publishing office, in Paris, dated March, 1943, addressed to Yolande. We must backtrack for one moment. Shortly after the tragic events of Venoix, Yolande had gathered together her husband's articles and poems (leaving aside the prison notes and letters out of prudence), these forming a small volume that she had clandestinely printed under the title *Writings of Joseph Bridet (1908-1941), Who Died for his Country.*

The German functionary writing to Yolande asked her why she had gone to the trouble of publishing in secret a small volume which could just as well have been brought out openly and wherein there was nothing to be found that was offensive to Germany. He ended rather ponderously by saying that his compatriots were not in the habit of opposing any demonstration aiming, without any political ulterior motive, at perpetuating the memory of the departed.